The
Silver Spoon
of
Solomon Snow

The
Silver Spoon
of
Solomon Snow

KAYE UMANSKY

CANDLEWICK PRESS
CAMBRIDGE, MASSACHUSETTS

Copyright © 2004 by Kaye Umansky
Frontispiece copyright © 2005 by Scott Nash

First U.S. edition 2005

Library of Congress Cataloging-in-Publication Data

Umansky, Kaye.
The silver spoon of Solomon Snow / Kaye Umansky. — 1st U.S. ed.
p. cm.
Summary: Ten-year-old Solomon Snow, a foundling who was discovered with a distinctive silver spoon in his mouth, sets out to find his parents and receives help along the way from an aspiring writer, a precocious young circus performer, and several orphans.
ISBN 0-7636-2792-5
[1. Foundlings—Fiction. 2. Friendship—Fiction. 3. Identity—Fiction. 4. Spoons—Fiction.] I. Title.
PZ7.U363Sil 2005
[Fic]—dc22   2005045788

2 4 6 8 10 9 7 5 3 1

Printed in the United States of America

This book was typeset in Columbus.

Candlewick Press
2067 Massachusetts Avenue
Cambridge, MA 02140

visit us at www.candlewick.com

For Caroline Sheldon, my wonderful agent

How It Began

In which the Intelligent Reader
learns of the strange
and unfortunate beginnings
of Solomon Snow.

ᏋᎷᎧPicture it. A howling black night on a high, lonely moor. Bitter winds roar across the angry sky, lashing the land with snow. Drifts pile into peaks. Trees crack. Rivers freeze. All in all, a bit of a nasty night.

At the very top of the moor, where a few stunted trees provide no shelter whatsoever, sits a small, tumbledown cottage. It's more of a hovel really, with an attached pigsty, which is currently unoccupied and rapidly filling with snow.

No one lives here, surely? You would have to be either desperate or a complete idiot to live here. Wouldn't you?

But wait. There is a thin trickle of smoke rising from the chimney. And isn't that a dim light—coming from behind the sagging shutters?

Yes. People do indeed live here. They are called the Scubbinses and they run a local washing and drying service.

A new sound joins in harmony with the whistling wind. It is the crunch of approaching wheels.

Here comes a cart, slowly grinding up the slippery slope, pulled by a straining horse. The driver is hunched over, well muffled in a long cloak. A big snow-covered wicker basket is rattling around in the back of the cart.

The horse finally makes it to the top and comes to a halt before the cottage. It waits, gently steaming, while the muffled figure climbs down, goes to the side of the cart, and hoists the large wicker basket into his arms.

Staggering a bit, buffeted by the wind, he carries the basket up to the cottage door and, with a grunt, deposits it on the doorstep. After a moment, his footsteps crunch away. After a short pause, there comes the sound of the cart moving off.

There sits the basket, in the snow. It has a lid, so we can't see inside. If we could, we would know that it is full of items of superior clothing. Lacy, frilly things. Velvets. Satins. Rich folks' clothes. And something else. Something alive.

A baby. A boy.

And in his mouth is a silver spoon.

Inside the hovel, Arnold Scubbins knocks out his pipe in the fireplace, stands up, and says to his wife, "I think it's easing off. Reckon I'll pop down to the tavern for a pint." ༄

I Hate It,
and the Toilets Smell

In which the Intelligent Reader
is introduced to Solomon Snow

and Prudence Pridy, who

meet by chance in the lane,

share a crust, and moan a lot.

Solomon Snow was walking along a quiet country lane, minding his own business, thinking vague thoughts, when a voice spoke in his ear, almost making him jump out of his boots.

"Where are you going, boy?" said the voice.

Solly looked up. Poking down at him from between the leaves of a chestnut tree was a nose.

Uh-oh. His heart sank. He knew that nose. It was attached to that weird Prudence Pridy from the village. Eldest daughter of the local poacher, who was currently in jail. (Again.) Usually had her unfortunate appendage buried in a book, because the village boys sang a rude song about it. Not that he'd ever joined in, of course.

What did she want with him?

Right now, she was perched on a branch, skinny legs dangling, an open composition book in her lap. A gnawed pencil stuck out of her ugly straw bonnet in a mad sort of way.

"What are you doing up there?" asked Solly rather gruffly. He wasn't used to talking to girls.

"Sitting," said Prudence.

"Oh. Right." He would have left it at that and continued on his way, but it wasn't to be.

"What's in your bundle?" demanded Prudence.

"Dirty washing," said Solly with a sigh. "Old Mother Rust's winter unmentionables."

He glanced at his bundle. Old Mother Rust's winter unmentionables only got washed once a year. He would be glad to get them home. He had a feeling they might burst into flames.

"Got anything to eat?"

Ah. Right. That's why she was talking to him.

"Well, just a bit of crust I'm saving for my dinner—"

"Stand back," ordered Prudence, stuffing her book into a handy hole in the trunk. "I'm coming down."

There was a flurry of brown and a shower of twigs and leaves. Seconds later, she stood before him, ankle deep in autumn leaves. Solly thrust his hand into his pocket, fingers closing protectively over his pathetically small hunk of bread.

Prudence Pridy was tall and gawky and seemed

to be built from knees and elbows. Everything about her was all wrong. Her boots were too big and her hat was too horrible, even without the pencil sticking out. Her dress was a brown shape-less sack. As for the nose—well. You only had to look. It was long. It was pointed. It ruled her face. You couldn't stop staring at it.

"Shouldn't you be in class?" asked Solly. Prudence, he knew, attended the village charity school, where you got free meals. He had seen her marching through the gates at the head of a long line of small, squabbling sisters.

"I'm not going to school anymore," said Prudence.

"Oh? Why not?" He hoped if he got her talk-ing, it might divert her mind to things other than the crust in his pocket. Besides, to tell the truth, he was curious. He had never been to school.

"Because I hate it, and the toilets smell." Prudence flicked her mousy braids and gave a haughty sniff. "Anyway, I know all I need to know. She can't teach me anything."

"Who, Miss Starch?" asked Solly, whose route occasionally took him past the playground. The village schoolmistress was stiff and scratchy, just like her name.

"Calls herself a teacher. I'd learn more in a school of fish."

"Ha, ha," chortled Solly politely. "A school of fish. That's a good one. Well, better be getting alo—"

"School!" spat Prudence, as though he hadn't spoken. "It's rubbish. We count to ten on our fingers. We recite baby rhymes about eggs on walls. We chant stupid sentences. 'My dog is in the bog. My rat is in the cat.'"

"Are they? Oh yes, I see what you—"

"She makes us stand on a stool in the corner wearing a dunce's hat. Like when I refused to be chalk monitor. And she makes us sew samplers. Mine says, 'Prudence Is Best.' She's made me unpick it seven times. I've been doing it for three years."

"Well, that's certainly a long t—"

"Three years!"

"I heard you the fir—"

"I loathe, despise, and detest sewing!"

Solly was surprised. He thought sewing was what girls did.

"So what do you like doing, then?" he asked. "If you don't like sewing?"

"Reading, mostly. When I get a chance."

"Oh. Right." As far as Solly was concerned, reading was right up there with wingless flight and indoor plumbing. It was something that would never happen to him.

"And eating," added Prudence.

Here it comes, thought Solly. She's homing in.

"Well," he said quickly, "I'd best make tracks. Nice talking to you. . . ." And he turned to walk away.

"I haven't had any breakfast," said Prudence. "Cleanliness spilled it on the cat."

Solly came to a halt.

"What? *Who?*"

"My baby brother, Cleanliness. Spoiled rotten because he's the only boy. Gets away with murder. I wanted Ma to call him Murderous, but she wouldn't. Look, can I have a bite of your bread or can't I? I just want to know, that's all."

There. Finally, she had come out with it.

Solly sighed. It was so unfair. He hadn't had any breakfast either. He had been looking forward to his dinner. But he couldn't really say no, could he? It would be too mean. He pulled out his precious crust, unwrapped it, and broke it in two.

"Here," he said, handing over half.

"Thanks."

Prudence plunked down on a fallen log, unveiled her rather horsy teeth, and started eating. After a moment's hesitation, Solly joined her. It would be rude to just walk off. Besides, he always sat down to eat. When you don't get much food, it's important to savor the scraps that come your way.

Automatically, he shook out the square of linen cloth his bread had been wrapped in and carefully tucked it into his shirt collar. He was fond of his cloth. He'd had it since he was a baby. He used it to wrap food and protect his shirt from crumbs and stains. He didn't like to be parted from it. He wouldn't let his mother wash it. He always insisted on doing it himself. He even slept with it, although nobody knew that.

He noticed Prudence staring and went a bit pink. But she didn't say anything.

For a time, they sat chewing in the weak autumn sunshine. The bread was very stale and required hard work in the jaw department.

After a bit, just to make conversation, he said, "Do you all have odd names in your family?"

"Yep." Prudence ticked them off on her fingers. "There's me, Faith, Hope, Charity, Joy, Delight, Patience, Grace, and Cleanliness."

"And are they? You know—joyful and delightful and clean and all that?"

"Oh, no. They're vile. They fight like piranha fish."

"Do *you* fight like a banana fish?" asked Solly. He was an only child. He didn't know how big families worked.

"I rise above it. And it's *piranha*. You're Solomon Snow, aren't you?"

"Solly," said Solly.

"You live in that cottage up on the moor. Your ma takes in washing, right?"

"Yes."

"Must be nice living up there with no one to bother you. Do you like it?"

"It's all right. A bit dull, actually."

"Why?"

Questions, questions, thought Solly. Why all these questions? She really was nosy, in more ways than one. Mind you, it was quite a novelty. Nobody had ever shown much interest in him before.

"No one to talk to, except sheep," he told her.

"Better than the village, at any rate," said Prudence. "Full of gossips, the village. Always running to tell my ma they've seen me with a book."

"What's in the books you read?" asked Solly.

"All kinds of stuff. Stories."

"What about?"

"People going on dangerous adventures and seeking their destiny. It helps if there's a good, juicy murder."

Solly was surprised at this. He thought girls liked stuff about flowers and fairies.

A small bird with a worm in its beak came hopping up, head to one side. Prudence threw it a crumb. It dropped the worm, scooped up the crumb, and took to the sky.

"Wish I could do that," she said with a little sigh.

"What—hop on one leg and eat worms?"

He thought it was funny—well, funny-ish—but Prudence obviously didn't.

"No," she said. "Fly. I wouldn't hang around here—that's for sure. I'd make a beeline for Town."

Town, eh? Solly had never been to Town. He'd heard tales about it, of course. He knew all about the shops, the taverns, the gas lamps, the smoking chimneys, and the cobbled streets heaving with rogues and pickpockets. It sounded very exciting—although people said it was highly dangerous in places. Not that he'd ever find out. Town was impossibly far away. Two days' ride, at least. That's if you had a horse.

He wondered why Prudence wanted to go there. He felt sure it was no place for a young girl of tender years and a mile-long nose.

"Why Town?" he asked. "I thought you said you liked to be quiet, with no one to bother you."

"I have my reasons," said Prudence. Clearly, she didn't want to say what these were. Solly felt a bit annoyed. After all, she had just eaten half his dinner. He was just about to stand up and go, when Prudence suddenly asked, "Why are you called Snow?"

"Because that's my name."

"Yes, but why? It's not your parents' name, is it?"

This was true. Solly's ma and pa were called Scubbins.

"That's a bit odd, isn't it?" Prudence asked. "Calling your son by a different last name?"

"No, it's not," argued Solly. She was a fine one to talk about names. Though, actually, come to think of it, she had a point. It was a bit odd. He had never really thought about it before. Your name was just one of those things you grew up with. Besides, Ma and Pa were hardly what you would call worldly-wise. They probably didn't realize you were supposed to call your child after you.

"Well, I think it's very strange," said Prudence. "If I were you, I'd ask them about it. You never know—you might turn out to be a foundling."

"A what?"

"A foundling. A baby that's found. Like in *Little Sir Thummagain*."

"Come again?"

"No, Thummagain. It's a story. You see, this baby's left in a box on the doorstep of these poor people, the Scums, and they call him Bugless and bring him up as their own. And quite by accident, he finds out he's really Sir Toby Thummagain, son of Lord Royston Thummagain, this rich nobleman, who—"

"How?" interrupted Solly.

"What?"

"Bugless. How did he find out?"

"There was a silk handkerchief with his true initials on it. It was in the box he came in."

"How old was he? When he found the handkerchief?"

"I don't know. Ten or eleven."

"And they hadn't thrown the box out in all that time?"

"They were poor. They used it for keeping the coal in."

Solly thought about this. It all sounded pretty unlikely.

"How does it end?" he asked.

"I haven't gotten to that. I expect he'll fulfill his destiny and get reunited with his true father and get to wear purple velvet pantaloons."

"Oh, right," said Solly. He wasn't sure what pantaloons were, but he didn't like the sound of them. He thought of something else. "What about the Scums? Will he go back and visit them?"

"I don't know. Why? Should he?"

"Well, they took him in."

"Only because they needed the box."

"Hmm." Solly had finished his crust. He reached for his trusty cloth and used it to dab his lips. He noticed Prudence staring again. He hastily stuffed the cloth back in his pocket, reached for his bundle (which was beginning to attract flies), and stood up.

"You've got good manners for a washer boy, haven't you?" said Prudence suddenly.

"I don't know. Have I? Sorry."

"No, no, it's a good thing. Makes for a nice change around here. You're off, then."

"Yep. Got to get home. Ma's waiting for this. I'll get it if I'm late."

"Well—thanks for breakfast. If anyone asks, you haven't seen me, right?"

"Right." Solly nodded. He paused. "Well— good luck with the—um—reading. You can tell me what happens to Bugless next time I see you. When you've finished the book."

"All right. Bye, then."

"Bye."

He trudged away, reflecting that that was the most interesting conversation he'd ever had with a girl. Well, actually, to be honest, the only conversation. The village children tended to ignore him, probably because he lived way up on the moor. The only time he saw them was when he was trudging past with bags of washing. Sometimes, girls would pause in their skipping games and giggle when he walked by. But they never spoke to him.

Prudence really wasn't that bad. At least she was a non-giggler. All that book-reading had turned her head a bit, but that was a good story, about Bugless Scum. All those new words and funny-sounding names. *Destiny. Pantaloons.* And what was that word again? *Foundlet? Findling?* He'd never come across it before.

He glanced back over his shoulder as he rounded the corner. She was already back up the tree with her composition book out, scribbling away and frowning.

Yes. She was all right.

Shame about the nose, though.

There Was a Spoon, Son

❧

In which the Intelligent Reader
makes the acquaintance of the Scubbinses,
pottage is explained, and Solly
discovers some vital information
about his background.

M

a," said Solly. "Why am I named Snow?"

It was evening, and they were sitting at the supper table eating pottage. This is a sort of vegetable slop that sticks to your teeth and tastes like boiled stinging nettles. They had it every night except on Turnip Sundays, which were even worse if you didn't like turnips.

"Why not?" said his ma. "Something wrong with your name now? Don't you like it?"

"Well, yes, but—"

"There you are, then! More pottage, Pa? It's lovely."

"Ar," said her husband. "Plop it in."

Ma Scubbins picked up the pot and dumped a load of goo into Pa's wooden bowl. Pa raised it to his lips, slurped long and revoltingly, dragged a dirty hand across his wet mustache, and said, "Wind's comin' up." Then he burped. Which was what he always did.

Ma dumped the empty pot on its side on the floor. A thin cat sidled up from nowhere, stuck its head in the pot, and began to lick. Solly winced. He hated the way Ma always let the cat wash up.

"Go on, Son," said Ma. "Eat up. That's lovely, that is."

Dully, Solly eyed the mess in his bowl and wished for the umpteenth time that he had a spoon to eat it with. Just a spoon—that's all. But the Scubbinses were very basic people. They didn't use cutlery. Still, at least he had managed to slip his crumb-catching cloth onto his lap without anyone noticing. (Ma and Pa always teased him about his cloth. It was high on the list of what they called Solly's Fancy Ways.)

He lifted the bowl of pottage to his lips and sipped.

Yep. Horrible as always.

Steam hung in the air, as it always did after a big wash. A battered wicker basket and an ancient scrubbing board were propped up by the stone sink. Through the window, he could see the washing line, which was currently filled with Old Mother Rust's winter unmentionables. Scratchy gray vests, scary gray corsets, and vast gray bloomers, silhouetted in all their glory against the darkening sky. Twenty-three items in all. He knew. He'd hung them out.

Hanging out the washing was one of his jobs. Along with slopping the pig, chopping logs, fetching water, keeping the fire lit and the water boiling, folding sheets, chasing the cat away from the pottage pot, and running a twenty-four-hour delivery service while vainly trying to instill some basic hygiene in the place. Not that anybody cared.

Pa certainly didn't. He never lifted a finger. Right now, he was stuffing tobacco into a large, smelly old clay pipe. He always had a pipe of tobacco after a hard day of sitting in a chair resting his back. Pa had had a weak back for as long as Solly could remember. He claimed it ran in the family. Helping fold a sheet could lay Pa up for a week, although he always miraculously recovered whenever he walked down to the tavern, which was most nights.

"Hurry up, Son," said his mother. "There's still the sheets to fold."

Solly forced down his pottage, looking around for something to take his mind off the taste.

The cottage had two rooms. Upstairs was for sleeping. It contained the parental bedroom, which was little more than a hayloft. Above that was a tiny space up under the roof, where Solly slept. Downstairs was for everything else. The low-beamed room in which they currently sat served as kitchen, laundry, dining room, and living room all rolled into one.

Tools, clothing, and a few kitchen implements hung from hooks on the walls. There was little else, apart from the washing stuff, the blackened range, and a few sticks of furniture. Straw was strewn about the floor, to mop up the grease and make the pig feel at home whenever it wandered in.

A small fire smoldered cheerlessly in the hearth. Next to it was a pile of damp logs and an almost empty coal box.

"Ma," said Solly.

"Now what?" Ma Scubbins had taken out her mending box and was darning a sock by the light of a candle stub. Pa was concentrating on working up a fog of smoke with his pipe. The wind sighed in the chimney.

"The old coal box. Where did it come from?"

"Bless us, boy, how should I know? The market, probably. Why? What's wrong with the coal box?"

"Nothing," said Solly. "It reminded me of a story somebody told me—that's all. About some baby

that was left on the doorstep in a box. It was a—
what was it again? Flounder. No, hang on, that's a
fish. I mean a"—he cast about for the right word,
then seized upon it triumphantly—"a *foundling*!"

He wasn't prepared for the effect the word had
on his audience.

Pa choked on his pipe.

Ma gasped and dropped the sock.

The cat started coughing up a hairball.

"What?" said Solly. "What did I say?"

"Who told you such a thing?" demanded Ma.

"Prudence Pridy from the village."

"What, the poacher's daughter? I might have
known. She's got no business runnin' around pokin'
her great nose into people's affairs, has she, Pa?"

"I'm goin' for a pint," said Pa, getting up from
his chair.

"You'll do no such thing! You tell Solly not to
talk to that Pridy girl ever again. Tellin' great lies.
Makin' things up."

"That's the whole point of stories, Ma,"
explained Solly. "They're made up. What are you
getting so worked up about?"

"Well, she should get her facts straight! Sayin' it

were a box, indeed, when everyone knows it were a basket—"

She broke off, gave a little gasp, and clapped her hand over her mouth.

"Oh my!" she whispered. "What have I gone an' said!"

There came a sudden gust of wind. The door blew open. A tangle of bracken blew in. It bowled slowly across the floor, coming to rest in the fireplace.

"A basket?" asked Solly into the deathly silence.

No one spoke. Ma sat frozen in horror. Pa stood vaguely hovering halfway between his chair and the door. Solly's eyes moved slowly from one to the other.

"Am I to take it," he said, pronouncing every word very clearly, "that I was left on the doorstep in a basket?"

"Yes!" wailed his mother. She buried her head in her apron. "Yes! Yes!"

"'Ere we go," muttered Pa to no one in particular.

"It's true! It's all true!" moaned Ma, rocking to and fro, shoulders heaving. "Oh, Solly, Solly! Don't be angry with Mother! I told Pa we should 'ave told you, right from the start. The truth will come out, I said."

"There you go, blamin' me," muttered Pa.

"Well, who am I to blame, then?" snapped Ma. She turned her red, swollen face to Solly. "You see, Son, we needed someone to help out, what with Pa's back and the Carter overcharging for deliveries."

"An' you needed a new washin' basket," Pa reminded her.

"Well, yes, there was that. And one night there were a terrible snowstorm—ooh, such a blizzard it were—an' Pa said he'd go for a pint."

Yes, thought Solly. He would.

"So he goes to the door, and there was the washin' basket, out on the step in all that snow. And we opens it up, and there you was. That's why we called you Solomon Snow, see, Solly. Because—"

"Because it was snowing. . . . Yes, I'd worked that out." Solly pointed to the old basket by the sink. "You don't mean—that washing basket?"

"Yes."

Solly shot up, sending his chair flying. He strode to the basket, snatched it up, and eagerly examined it for clues. Nothing, of course. It was just the same old wicker basket. It had been there forever. He'd handled it hundreds of times.

"You looked so sweet, tucked in under the fancy clothes," sniveled Ma.

"Ahem!" Pa gave a warning cough. "That's enough."

"Fancy clothes? What fancy clothes?" asked Solly.

"Yer ma's upset, Son," said Pa. "She don't know what she's sayin'."

But there was no stopping Ma now.

"Oh, such fine clothes they was, Son. Silk shirts with ruffles, and a lovely pair of velvet trousers. Pa got three shillings for 'em at the market, didn't you, Pa?"

"You sold my *clothes*?"

Solly's voice came out in a strangled squeak.

"They wasn't strickly your clothes, Son," said Pa. "You was a baby. They was too big for you."

"Still! They were in *my* basket. My clothes. My basket. Wasn't there anything else there? Any sort of clue to my identity? A note? An embroidered hankie? Didn't you even make *inquiries*?"

"No, Son. Brutally speakin', you was just plain dumped," said his father. "And we took you in, out of the kindness of our 'earts."

"And because you needed the basket."

"Well, yes, there was that."

"There must have been *something*," insisted Solly. "It was snowing. Wasn't I wrapped in a shawl or anything?"

"Nope. Just the cloth."

"Cloth? What cloth?"

"That bit of old cloth you drag round with you. It was newer then, o' course."

"I was wrapped in my *crumb-catching cloth*?"

"Aye."

Well, well. It was all coming out now. Solly snatched up his cloth, which had fallen to the floor. He stood turning it over in his hands. Just a plain, blank square, fraying a little on one edge, with a couple of stubborn grease stains that wouldn't come out. No clues there.

"How old was I at the time?" he demanded.

"Well, we don't know, do we?" sniffed his mother. "I do know you was teethin' because you had the spoon in yer mouth—"

She stopped and clapped her hand to her mouth again.

"Spoon?" said Solly. "What spoon?"

"*Now* see," muttered Pa Scubbins to his wife. "That's another can o' worms you've opened up."

"Oh, he might as well know it all," cried Ma Scubbins. She raised her sodden face to Solly. "There a was a spoon, Son. A fancy silver spoon. You was suckin' on it."

I can't believe this, thought Solly. Revelation after revelation! Doorstep, snow, cloth, basket, fancy clothes—and now a *spoon*?

"Well, there you are, then," he cried. "There might be—I don't know—a crest or a coat of arms on it or something. Let's see it, then. Where is it?"

"Ah," said his father. There was a pause.

"'Ah' as in 'Ah, we sold it'?" inquired Solly through gritted teeth. Were they completely crazy?

"Not quite."

"Threw it away? Lost it?" He was really shouting now. "Broke it? Used it to—to paddle up Mad River?"

"All right, no need to be snarky," said Pa rather sulkily. "We pawned it, if you must know."

"I don't believe this!" Solly thumped on the table. "I'm a foundling! Ten years you've kept this from me! Ten years and I suddenly find out we're not related!" At this, Ma burst into fresh sobs. Pa just looked a bit sheepish.

"Not only that," went on Solly, "not only that, but now you tell me I came with a spoon! A spoon! I could have eaten my pottage with that!"

"Don't be cross, Son," wailed his mother. "We let you keep yer bit o' cloth—"

"You pawned my silver spoon!"

"We had to! How else could we buy you boots?"

"I only got boots last November," Solly reminded her. It was true. He had gone barefoot for nine years. "And they're too small."

"But that's when we pawned the spoon! When you nearly lost yer toe to frostbite. We didn't want to, Solly. We was goin' to give it to you when you was grown and explain everythin', but you so wanted those boots. Pestered fer weeks, you did. In a way, it's yer own fault it went to the pawnshop."

"What pawnshop? Where?"

"In Town. Pa hitched a lift with Carter the Carter. When he was away that time. You thought he was goin' to see the apothecary about his back, remember? And a week later, he came home an' surprised you with the boots. Only three owners. Oh, you was that pleased! Until you tried them on. I did tell Pa to get big ones, but—"

"Have you still got the pawn ticket?"

"Er—no," confessed his father, scratching his head sheepishly. "I think I might 'ave lost it on the way home."

"On the way into the tavern," Ma said grimly.

"Do you remember where the shop is?" persisted Solly. "Got an address or anything?"

"Er—no."

"Well, that's great!" said Solly. "Just great! Thank you so much."

"That's all right, Son," said Pa. "Anything else we can do, just ask. Well, now that's all cleared up, I think I'll just pop on down an' 'ave a quiet p—"

"Hold it right there! Think. Think hard. This is important. What was the spoon like? Big? Small? What?"

"Spoon-size," said Pa. "An' shaped like a spoon. An' silver. That's about it, really."

"With fancy stuff carved on the handle," added Ma.

"Fancy stuff?" said Solly. His ears pricked up. "What fancy stuff?"

"Well—shapes. Fancy shapes."

"What, letters or something?"

"I dunno, Son. Coulda been. 'Ard to say."

Ah. Right. Of course. How would they know? They couldn't read either. Oh, well. They had told him all they could. There was nothing else to be done.

Solly snatched his cap from a peg and marched to the door.

"Where are you going, Son?" wailed his ma.

"I'm going to say goodbye to the pig."

"Goodbye? What do you mean, goodbye? Where are you going?"

"Where do you think? To get my spoon!"

"What—tonight?"

"Yes, tonight. Right now."

"But we haven't folded the sheets!"

Solly marched out, slamming the door behind him.

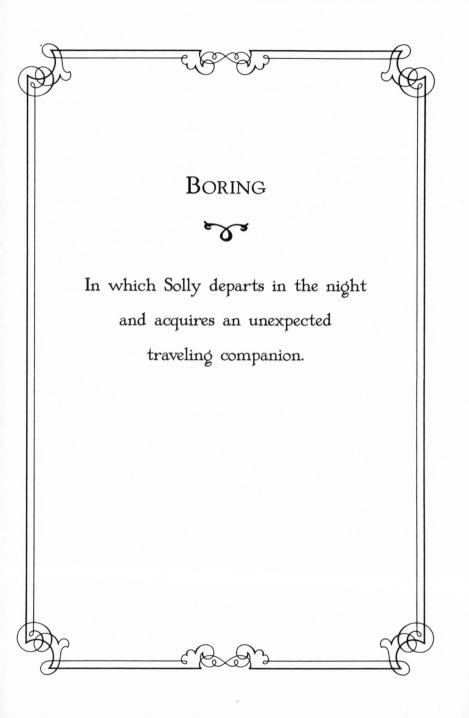

BORING

In which Solly departs in the night
and acquires an unexpected
traveling companion.

A huge yellow moon hung in the sky as Solly strode down the familiar track that linked the family homestead to the village of Boring. Yes. That was its name. Not Boring-on-the-Green, or Boring-by-the-Bridge, or even Boring-in-the-Mire. Just plain Boring, which summed it up perfectly.

It was a cold night. Autumn was turning to winter, and the wind whistled keenly through his threadbare jacket. Not that he cared. Right now, he was hot. Hot with fury.

His head rang with new words. Words like *dumped, foundling,* and *lied to for years.* Horrible words like that. And to think he'd never guessed any of it until some random girl told him a made-up story! How could he have been so stupid? How could he have missed all the clues? There were enough of them. Mentally, he made a list of all the things that should have given him pause for thought, if he'd had half a brain.

There was his name, for a start. Why had he never thought to ask about that?

Besides, he didn't even look like them. Ma was small and wiry, like a chicken, and Pa was plain fat. Solly was normal. He hadn't inherited Ma's wispy ginger hair or Pa's weak back. Solly's hair was dark brown and his back was just fine.

Then there was the question of his funny, finicky habits. Like stopping the cat from licking the pot and not feeding the pig at the table. Like washing his hands before eating. Like always removing his cap before sitting down. Like dabbing at his mouth with his crumb-catching cloth. Nobody else did those things.

Then there was the mysterious urge he always had to say "please" and "thank you." Not to mention his straw allergy and his deep-rooted dislike of pottage. . . .

Solly gave up the mental list. Everything pointed to the fact that the truth had been staring him in the face all his life and he'd never noticed until now. What a knucklehead.

His steel-capped boots struck sparks as he

strode along. A couple of panicked sheep took off at his approach, crashing through gorse bushes and bleating piteously.

"And good riddance to you, too!" shouted Solly.

A few minutes later, he slowed down. This was ridiculous. He'd be exhausted if he kept this up. He had to pace himself or he'd be starving in no time. Come to think of it, he was peckish already. He wished he'd finished the pottage.

Still. He'd shown them, all right. That was some exit he'd made. Serve them right if they missed him. He was boldly off to Town to claim his rightful spoon, so there.

He strode out again, swaggering a bit.

A bit farther along the way, he slowed down once more. Fury, righteous indignation, and boldness were giving way to a few practical considerations.

He had no food. No money. No pawn ticket. No address of the pawnshop. And no idea of the way. All he had were the clothes he stood in. Threadbare jacket, patched shirt, old cap, ragged breeches, and a pair of boots that pinched. At the very least he should have gone and gotten his winter sheepskin, instead of rushing out in such irresponsible clothing.

He fumbled inside his pockets. Nothing there, either. Except for his crumb-catching cloth.

He shook it out and examined it again. His cloth. All he had that was truly his. And to think that he had been wrapped in it as a baby. No wonder he was so attached to it. Well, from now on, he wouldn't hide it away, as though it were something to be ashamed of. He would wear it with pride.

Carefully, with reverent fingers, he folded it into a triangle, knotted it around his neck, and walked on.

As you might expect, Boring was sleeping. Here and there, candlelight glowed in a window, but mostly, everyone was in bed. It was the warmest place to be, this time of year. Curtains were firmly drawn. Doors were closed sternly against the night. Even the chained dogs were too bored to bark.

It felt strange to be up and about so late. The whole village seemed to radiate disapproval. His clattering footsteps echoed. He felt he should be tiptoeing along, but his boots weren't built for it.

Even the tavern was having a slow night, by the look of things. Subdued voices murmured from behind the closed door. Pa would be in there now if it was a normal night. But it wasn't, and Pa wasn't. He was back home comforting Ma and, he hoped, drowning in guilt.

Good.

He passed the silent schoolyard, where Miss Starch stood every day ringing the big bell. Then came the church and the surrounding graveyard. Solly quickened his step, crossing his fingers for luck and keeping his head turned well away from the ghostly headstones that loomed over the crumbling wall.

He passed the pond on the village green. He passed the horse trough, the smithy, and the cobblers. Then came the last few cottages before Boring fizzled out and became Big Scary Beyond. He had never ventured that far. Old Mother Rust's hovel along the lane was the extent of his travels. The Scubbinses' washing business was a very local affair.

There was only the one road out of Boring, so he couldn't go wrong. He would be fine following that. But what would he do if he came to a crossroads? Presumably, there would be a signpost. But he couldn't read, so how would he know which way to take? It really was very inconvenient, not knowing his letters.

He walked on. He had reached the last cottage now. That was where Prudence Pridy lived. If only she could see him now. Off to Town! Just like that! She'd be in bed now, side by side with her seven sisters and little monster of a brother, reading one of her books by candlelight, perhaps, never dreaming that he was passing by—

"Pssst!" hissed a voice from behind the hedge. "Solly!"

Solly nearly died. He looked wildly around as an angular shape emerged from the shadows.

"Prudence! What the—"

"Shhh! Keep your voice down!" said Prudence. She looked just the same as before, with the unhelpful addition of a shabby brown cloak.

"You nearly gave me a fit! What are you doing up?"

"Waiting for you, of course."

"But—how did you know I was coming?"

"I get a feeling about these things," said Prudence, sounding rather smug. "I knew you'd be along sooner or later. It's just the way things work."

"In your books, perhaps. Not in real life."

"You'd be surprised," said Prudence. "Life Mirrors Fiction. Don't you know that?"

"What?"

"I'll explain sometime. Besides, I heard you coming from miles away. Look, let's get going, shall we? They'll hear us if we stand here yakking."

"We? What d'you mean, we?"

"Us. You and me. We're running away to Town, aren't we? Oh, there's no need to look like that. I won't interfere with you. We'll split up when we get there. I just thought it'd be safer if we stuck together on the journey. You're more likely to get a lift if you've got me with you. People feel sorrier for girls. Everyone knows that."

Her sharp nose bobbed in the moonlight. Privately, Solly thought she was the last girl to get an offer of a lift on a cold night, but he didn't say so.

"You can't come," he said, abruptly turning away. "I'm sorry, but that's that."

"Why not?"

"Because your ma would go mad."

"No, she won't. Dad's in jail again, so no more rabbits for the pot. It's hard at home right now. I'll be one less mouth to feed. I don't suppose she'll even notice I'm gone."

"No," said Solly, quickening his pace. "It's impossible."

"I've got stuff for the journey," said Prudence. Her long, skinny legs were keeping up easily. For the first time, he noticed that she had a small basket in her hand.

"Like what?" said Solly, curious despite himself.

"Bread, cheese, apples. A crow-scarer, to raise the alarm in case we get attacked. A map. A candle, a box of matches, and a useful knife. A few private things of my own. And my life savings."

"How much?"

"Sixpence."

"You've thought of everything, haven't you?" said Solly. He tried to sound sneering, although, in fact, he was filled with grudging admiration at Prudence's forethought. If he'd had any sense, he would have brought—well, something.

"Pretty much."

"Everything except how you're going to persuade me to let you tag along."

"I am not tagging along!" snapped Prudence. They were almost running now. Both of them were beginning to puff a bit. "I'm here under my own steam. I don't suppose you've thought to bring anything, have you?"

"Well—"

"I thought not. I've been packed and ready to go for ages. It took me weeks to get everything together. Years, if you include saving up the sixpence. Besides, you need me."

"Oh, I do?"

"Certainly. Because you can't read, can you?"

"So?"

"So how will you know what the signposts say?"

"I'll get by," said Solly stiffly.

"How?"

"I'll ask."

"There might not be anyone around. Then you'll need a map. But, hey! You don't have a map, do you? And even if you did, you couldn't read it."

"Look!" Solly stopped running and turned on her. "I might not be able to read, as you keep pointing out, but there's more to me than you think. I'll have you know that I happen to be—" He stopped. Why was he bothering? It was none of her business anyway.

"What?" said Prudence.

"Never mind. Go home. Leave me alone."

"No. What? Go on. Tell."

"If you must know, I happen to be a flounder. Foundling, I mean," he corrected himself quickly.

"I knew it!" Prudence gave a self-satisfied nod. "I just knew it. I'd heard the gossip, of course, but—"

"Gossip? What gossip?"

"About you being dumped on the Scubbinses' doorstep. And I must say I never thought you were a Boring boy. You're different."

"I am?" Solly was all ears. "How, exactly?"

It would be fascinating to hear Prudence's take on the matter. Had she spotted noble qualities or something? Not that he was fishing for compliments or anything.

"Well," said Prudence, reflecting, "well, obviously, nobody likes you much. You don't fit in."

"Oh. I see. Well, thank you for that."

"Then there's other stuff you probably don't even notice about yourself. That napkin business you do."

"Napkin?"

"That cloth you use. I see you've taken to wearing it round your neck."

"What—my crumb-catching cloth?"

"Yep. Rich people have them, to protect their clothes. Round here, they eat like pigs in a trough. They all laugh at you about that. I didn't," she added hastily.

"So," said Solly. "Everyone knows I'm a foundling."

"Um, probably. Yes."

"Everyone but me."

"Um, yes."

"Well, that's just great." Solly aimed a bitter kick at the hedge. "No wonder they look at me in a weird way."

"I don't know what you're sulking about," said Prudence. "It's good news, isn't it? I mean, you're not just ordinary. You're a Man Of Mystery. Tell me the details—I want to know everything. Were you left in a box, like Bugless?"

"Not quite," said Solly.

"What, then? Tell."

"Well . . . all right, then, if you really want to know. . . ."

And before he knew it, he was telling her everything. About the snowstorm and the washing basket and the velvet trousers and—well, everything.

"So I'm going to track down my spoon," he finished. "It's my inheritance, and I want it. With any luck, it might lead me to my real parents. It's in a pawnshop in Town. That's all I know."

"Town's a big place, so I've heard," mused Prudence. "You haven't got the ticket, you say?"

"No. Pa lost it."

"Hmm. Tricky."

"I wonder what Bugless would do," said Solly.

They were walking again, following the now-moonlit lane where they had met that very morning. The village was behind them. They had almost reached Prudence's hiding tree. Soon, they would pass Old Mother Rust's hovel, and then— who knows?

"He'd look for the sign with the three balls," said Prudence promptly. "It'll be up a backstreet. They always are. There'll probably be a horrible old man with greasy hair and fingerless gloves. He'd be called Zebediah Stinge, or something like that."

"Do you think he'd insist on the ticket?"

"Sure to. Of course, chances are he'll have sold the spoon long ago. Pawnshops are supposed to hang on to stuff for a certain amount of time in case the owner comes back to redeem them, but they often don't."

"How do you know so much about these things?" asked Solly.

"It was in *The Curious Olde Pawne Shoppe.* Like I say, I read a lot. It makes me prepared for any eventuality."

"Well, good. Let's hope your books tell you what to do when you can't keep up with me and wake up in a ditch with rats nibbling your toes."

"Listen, Solomon Snow!" hissed Prudence. "Let's get this straight. We're sticking together until we get to Town. I can keep up with you any day. Another word and I'll rattle my crow-scarer." She put her hand into her basket.

"All right, all right!" said Solly. She meant it. He could tell.

Perfect Parents
Interlude One

In which the Intelligent Reader

takes a break from old friends

in order to be introduced to

a set of Perfect Parents.

Far away, on a grand country estate, Lady Elvira stood at the window in her silken nightgown, staring up at the moon. Her husband, Lord Charles, sat upright in bed, reading the paper by the light of his bedside candelabra. He wore a cotton nightcap and was idly combing his fine mustache with a small silver comb.

"Look at the moon, darling," Lady Elvira said with a sigh, dabbing at her eyes with a tiny lace hankie. "It's full tonight."

"So it is, dearest," said Lord Charles. "Come to bed. You'll catch a chill."

"Whenever I see the moon, I wonder whether it's shining down on our lost boy. Is it, Charles? Oh, is it?"

"Sure to be, my love." Lord Charles kept his voice patient, although they had a similar conversation every night. He wouldn't have minded, but each night when he would finally persuade his wife into bed, her feet would be like blocks of ice.

"Then what is he doing out at night? Has he no roof over his head?"

"Of course he has, my love. Of course he has."

"Then how can the moon shine down on him?"

"Some sort of skylight arrangement, I would think—" began Lord Charles, but he was drowned out by his wife's loud cry of anguish.

"Oh, Charles, Charles! Will we never find him?"

"Of course we will, my dear. Now, come to bed. You're just getting yourself upset again."

Lady Elvira gave another sigh and drew the heavy velvet drape across the window. Then, slowly, she glided to the bed. Lord Charles shuffled over and made room. Lady Elvira got in.

Yes. Her feet were freezing.

I's the Infant Pwodigy

❦

In which Solly and Prudence arrive
at the circus, Signor Madelini makes a
brief appearance, and the Infant Prodigy
has a temper tantrum.

The morning was cold, bright, and sparkling. It was the sort of perfect autumnal morning when birds sing, squirrels go nuts, shy little woodland creatures scuttle around preparing for hibernation, and even sheep look relatively cheerful.

Sadly, it was thoroughly ruined by the sound of harsh, blaring, banging music, played by the sort of band that really shouldn't.

A traveling circus was in full swing in a large field. A flag mounted on a pole by the gate read, MADELINI'S MARVELOUS EXTRAVAGANZA!

Signor Madelini himself stood by the gate, a money box at his elbow and a whip in his hand. He cut an impressive figure in a shiny red suit, top hat, and long riding boots. He had greasy black hair and a small waxed mustache, which looked as though someone had painted two tadpoles on his upper lip. Behind him, the band scraped, honked, and banged away. The tops of tents, stalls, and painted caravans could be seen poking up behind the hedge.

A group of runny-nosed, ragged country children stood in the lane, staring at the exotic stranger.

"Got-a penny?" snapped Signor Madelini. The children slowly shook their heads. "Then get-a lost-a." He jerked his thumb.

The children still stared. He raised his whip. The children backed away, then wandered on up the lane, looking wistfully over their shoulders.

"Roll up-a!" screamed Signor Madelini, cracking his whip. "Roll up-a! Thees way for the extravaganza! One-a penny get-a you een! One-a penny ees all! What treats I 'ave een store! Dancing-a 'orses! The Amazeeng-a Flambo, World-a Famous Eater of Fire-a! Zor, the Strongest-a Man Een the Universe-a! Mees Pandora Constantinople, who weel perform on the tight-a rope-a! Leetle Rosabella, the Eenfant Prodigy-a, who weel seeng-a for you and melt-a your heart!"

"Wow!" said Solly as they trudged up the lane. His weary eyes widened. "What's going on up ahead?"

"'Madelini's Marvelous Extravaganza,'" read Prudence. "So that's what's deafening everyone for miles around."

They both looked the worse for wear. Their eyes were bloodshot from lack of sleep. Their boots were covered with road dust. Solly's feet were really beginning to hurt now—unsurprising, considering that they had walked for the best part of the night, only stopping to catch forty winks by the roadside just before sunrise. They hadn't talked much, because they needed all their breath for walking.

Breakfast had been a grouchy, muttered affair. They had sloshed cold stream water over their faces and shared a shriveled apple. Solly had mumbled something hopeful about cheese, but Prudence said they should save it for later. It was her cheese, so he hadn't pressed the matter.

"I've never been to a circus," said Solly.

"Me neither," said Prudence. "I've read about them, of course."

"Of course," said Solly with a small sigh. She would have.

"Come!" screamed Signor Madelini, catching sight of them and beckoning invitingly. "Come, my leetle chickadees! Come and see the show-a! Dancing-a 'orses! One penny ees all!"

"I don't suppose we could—" began Solly.

"No," said Prudence.

"But I've always wanted to—"

"No. We can't afford it. We're going to walk straight past."

She was right, of course. But Solly couldn't help feeling terribly disappointed. A circus was temptation of the highest order.

They were just about to carry on, when:

"WAAAAAAAAAAAAAAAAAH!"

A sudden, terrible, high-pitched shriek arose from behind the hedge. Signor Madelini went pale. The awful music clattered to a confused halt. A flight of startled birds took off from a nearby tree. A dog began howling miles away.

A small girl shot into the lane. She was a vision in blue. She wore a blue dress, blue knee-length frilly knickers trimmed with blue lace, little blue boots, and a blue gauze bonnet tied with blue ribbons. She held a little blue parasol in her hand. The only thing about her that wasn't blue was her face, which was bright scarlet.

"Rosabella," said Signor Madelini soothingly. He bent down, hands on knees, and attempted a smile. "What ees wrong, *bambina*? Tell Uncle Mad-a. Why you so upset-a?"

The blue vision planted her two little feet

firmly in the road and scowled into his face. Then, quite deliberately, she drew back her dainty little parasol and rammed him in the stomach with the pointy end. At the same time, she stamped hard on his foot.

"Cripes!" gasped Solly. "Look at that!"

Signor Madelini doubled over, brow creased with pain. He hopped about in the road clutching his middle, while the blue vision looked on in satisfaction. She then gave another scream, lay down in the road, and pounded her little fists into the dirt.

"She's having a temper tantrum," said Prudence with a disapproving sniff. "Just like my sister Joy."

"She'll get it now, I'll bet," said Solly. But she didn't.

"Rosabella, Rosabella!" wailed Signor Madelini, finally recovering enough to talk. "Why-a you be such a bad-a girl? Why-a you do thees to poor Uncle Mad, uh?"

But the blue vision wasn't telling. She shot up, stamped her little foot, stuck out her bottom lip, turned on her heel, and flounced off down the lane, golden curls bouncing.

"Rosabella!" beseeched Signor Madelini. "*Bellissima!* Come-a back-a!"

"Go away!" shouted the blue vision over her shoulder. "I hate you! You's howwid! Leave me alone!"

"Mamma mia!" groaned Signor Madelini, clutching his head. "What I do to deserve-a thees?"

"Come on," said Prudence, tugging at Solly's arm. "Let's go. Remember, ignore the sales pitch."

And they hurried past the gate. Signor Madelini was so taken up with the rapidly receding blue vision that he didn't even look at them.

"Honestly," said Prudence as they got out of earshot, "I thought Joy was bad enough, but that little blue brat takes the—oh!"

They rounded the corner and very nearly tripped over the brat herself. She was sitting in the middle of the lane, using the tip of her frilly parasol to stab holes in the packed dirt. Solly and Prudence drew up short and stared down. The small girl's face was fading from scarlet to rosy pink. Up close, they could see she had huge, melting blue eyes with long lashes. A sweet, simpering, gap-toothed smile rose to her rosebud lips, her cheeks dimpled, and she said, "Hello. Has you got any sweeties?"

"No," said Prudence.

"Sorry," added Solly to soften the blow. She did have very blue eyes. Prudence gave him a sideways glare.

"Oh," said the small girl sadly. "I was hopin' you had."

"Even if we did, why should we give them to you?" said Prudence.

"'Cause I like them. And they won't give me any." The small girl's lower lip trembled.

"Why won't they?" Solly asked. He felt quite sorry for her, being so deprived, although he'd never eaten a sweet in his life.

"'Cause they's howwid. They makes me eat gweens. I hate gween food. Uncle Mad says I's gettin' too fat an'll lose my teef."

"Come on," muttered Prudence. "We're wasting time."

"I's not fat, is I?" the small girl appealed to Solly.

"No," said Solly. "Certainly not." Although she was, in fact, quite round.

"I like you," said the small girl, flashing her dimples. "You is a nice boy. Do you fink I's pwetty?"

"No, he doesn't," snapped Prudence before

Solly could reply. "He thinks you're a silly showoff. Come on, Solly."

She hauled on his arm, but Solly resisted. The small girl fascinated him. He had never seen anyone so dressed up before. He didn't like to leave her sitting so sadly in the dirt in her blue finery.

"Is that your name?" asked the small girl, ignoring Prudence and concentrating all her efforts on Solly. "Solly? That's a nice name. I's Little Wosabella, the Infant Pwodigy. Where you goin', Solly?"

"He's going to Town, if it's any of your business," said Prudence.

"I isn't speakin' to you. I is speakin' to Solly."

The Prodigy climbed to her feet, shook the dust off her blue dress, and placed a small, trusting hand in Solly's. Her big blue eyes swam up at him. She batted her long lashes and said, "Can I come?"

"Oh, per-leez!" muttered Prudence. Her own small, mud-brown eyes rolled to heaven.

"Um, no," said Solly, trying to disengage his hand. The Prodigy had an unexpectedly strong grip.

"But I like Town. You can get sweeties there. I get 'em fwee, 'cause I's pwetty. The wed ones is best. I'll give you some—you can have the gween ones. I hate gween."

"I think I'm going to be sick," said Prudence.

"Not her, though," added the Prodigy.

"Listen," said Solly, finally prying her off. "I really think you should go back to your uncle now."

"Why, Solly?"

"Because you're too young to go off on your own."

"No I's not. 'Sides, I got you to pwoteck me." The Prodigy stared up from under her eyelashes and smiled her sweetest smile.

"Solly," said Prudence between clenched teeth. "Let's go. Now."

"Yes, all right, I'm coming. Look, er—"

"Wosabella."

"Yes. Look, Rosabella. I've got to go, see? I'm on a sort of—quest."

"Don't you like me, Solly?" The voice quavered. The blue eyes filled with tears.

"Yes, yes, I like you fine. But you can't come. So toddle on back to your uncle, all right?"

He gave the Prodigy's bonneted head an awkward little pat, turned on his heel, and hurried to catch up with Prudence, who was stalking off down the lane.

"What a hideous child," spat Prudence. She was scowling horribly, and the sharp end of her nose had gone pink.

"Oh, I don't know," said Solly. He thought about the little blue girl and the way she had put her trusting hand into his, then held on with the unexpected grip of iron. "Nice hair," he added unwisely.

"She's awful. I don't know why you even bothered talking to her. Children like that should be ignored, not encouraged."

"I didn't encourage her."

"Oh no? So why is she following us, then?"

Solly glanced over his shoulder. Prudence was right. The Prodigy was trotting up the lane behind them, curls bouncing, a determined look on her pink face. She caught him looking and waved her little blue parasol.

"Yoo-hoo! Solly! Wait for me!"

"She'll get tired in a minute," said Solly.

Little did he know.

PERFECT PARENTS
INTERLUDE TWO

In which the Perfect Parents
have breakfast and continue to
bemoan their missing child.

"More coffee, Charles?" inquired Lady Elvira, hand poised gracefully over the coffeepot.

"Thank you dearest, I will." Her husband spoke from behind the paper. They were having a late breakfast. Barnacle, the faithful old family servant, hovered in the background, quietly clearing away the numerous silver dishes set out on the long side tables.

"Any news today, dear?" Lady Elvira's voice trembled slightly.

"I'm afraid not, darling."

"Ah me." Her Ladyship rose and went to the window. She looked out over the rolling lawns, where a team of gardeners was busy clipping shrubs and pruning trees. Tears rose to her eyes. "Will we ever find him, Charles? Will we?"

"Come and drink your coffee, darling," urged her husband. "It's getting cold. We'll find him one day—I'm sure of it."

"But when? Ten years we've been looking. Ten years, and not even a sighting of the spoon! How many spoons have we looked at now?"

"Hundreds," said her husband in tones of deepest gloom.

"Ten missed birthdays!" quavered her Ladyship. "All those unopened gifts. He'll be too old for them now. The wooden duck on the string. The sweet little satin knicker-bockers. And the miniature pony's getting quite geriatric."

"I know, dearest, I know."

"Look at the sky, Charles. The clouds are gathering. Do you think they're gathering over the head of our boy?"

"Well, if they are, he can always put a hat on."

"But he may not have a hat! Oh, Charles, Charles! Suppose he doesn't even have a hat to cover his sweet head! What if he's out in the rain with no hat and no boots? What then?"

"There, there. Look, why not go and play the piano? You know it calms you down."

"Perhaps I will. But, oh! If only I knew where he is now!"

She's Awful

෨

In which Solly and Prudence acquire
an unwelcome addition to their party
and sharp words are exchanged.

I t's no good," said Solly. "I've got to take my boots off."

He slowed to a halt. His feet were killing him. They had been walking nonstop for hours, up hill and down dale. The winding road seemed to go on forever, past dull, endless fields and dull, empty woods. They had seen nobody, apart from a distant shepherd up on a hill, keeping watch over his dreary sheep. Once, some farm dogs had barked at them and a cow had given them a funny look, but apart from that, nothing.

"All right," said Prudence. "We should eat, anyway."

She sat on the grass verge and rummaged around in her basket. She had been distant all day. Solly had attempted a few conversational remarks from time to time, mainly about the sameness of the scenery and the agony of walking in too-tight boots, but she remained silent and sniffy, so in the end he had given up.

A small brook ran alongside the road. Solly flopped down next to it, hauled off his boots and wool stockings, which were more hole than stockings, and examined his feet.

"I've got blisters on the blisters on my blisters," he complained. Prudence shrugged and just carried on rummaging. No sympathy there. With a sigh, he lowered his throbbing feet into the water.

"Ouch!"

"Now what?"

"It's cold. They hurt."

"You do moan a lot, don't you? Don't you have anything but moany words in your vocabulary?"

"What's voca—what's that mean?"

"*Vocabulary.* The words you know. Yours seems to consist of nothing except 'ouch' and 'ooh my feet' and 'I'm hungry.'"

"Well, I'm very sorry if my boots hurt. Can we have some cheese now, please?"

"I'm getting it, I'm getting it. You're just like my sister Patience. No self-restraint. Goes mad if she can't have something then and there."

"I'm not going mad. I'd just like a bit of cheese, that's all," said Solly.

Honestly, he thought. She's so—prickly.

"It's coming, all right? Here."

Prudence hacked off a lump and threw it at him. It fell short and landed on the grass. Solly picked it up, wiped it off, and untied his trusty crumb-catcher. What had she called it again? Ah, yes. Napkin. He was a Foundling with a Napkin. So many new words. He had to admit that being with Prudence improved your Vocabulary. (That was another one.)

"How much farther, do you think?" he asked, spreading his *napkin* on his lap and placing the cheese on it.

"Miles."

"Of course, we might get a lift."

"Might."

"Look," said Solly, "what is it with you? You've hardly said a word all day."

"That's because I'm very disappointed in you."

"Why? What have I done?"

"Nothing but complain. And make an idiot of yourself with that stupid girl."

"How did I make an idiot of myself? I just talked to her for a minute—that's all. It's a free world. I can talk, can't I?"

Very deliberately, Prudence stood up, picked up her basket, and stomped off to sit under a tree with her back to him.

Solly took a bite of the cheese. It was very hard. He had a feeling it might have come from a mousetrap. He chewed and swallowed. It scratched a bit, going down. He glanced across at Prudence. She had taken the pencil from her bonnet and was bent over her composition book, tapping her teeth and looking thoughtful.

"I can talk!" he shouted again. No response.

Sighing, he finished his cheese and dabbed at his mouth with his napkin, which he then used to blot his feet. He tied it around his neck, pulled on his ruined stockings, eased his feet back into the boots, laced them, and stood up, trying not to groan.

Stoically, he limped over to Prudence, who pretended not to notice.

"Prudence?" he said.

"What?"

"Thanks for the cheese. Look, I'm, er, sorry if I upset you."

A pause. Then, "'S all right."

"What?"

"I said it's all right."

"So we're speaking again?"

"I suppose so."

"Right. Good. So"—Solly cast around for something to speak about that wouldn't end in a fight—"So. What are you writing? A diary or something?"

"No," said Prudence. She snapped the book shut, slipped it into her basket, and jabbed her pencil back into her bonnet.

"What, then?"

"Just notes. Look, I really think we should get on. We can get a few more miles behind us before night. We'll find a barn or something. I don't fancy sleeping in the open again. It's about to rain." Briskly, she stood up.

"Right. Good idea."

"Just one thing. Don't waste time picking up waifs and strays. We've got to stay focused."

"I didn't pick up any waifs and strays."

"Only because I stopped you. All she had to do was bat her eyelashes."

"Oh, come on. Look, we shook her off, didn't we?"

"Eventually. She was following us for miles. I

can still hear those silly little blue boots, tippy-tapping away—"

Suddenly, she broke off and clutched at his arm.

"What?" said Solly.

"Shh! Listen! Don't you hear it? Or am I going mad?"

Solly listened. A sound came to his ears. Relentless footsteps, approaching fast. *Tippy-tap, tippy-tap,* they went.

"Hello, Solly!" trilled a familiar voice. "It's me. I finded you."

And around the corner trotted the Prodigy!

She treated Solly to a gap-toothed beam. Her teeth were stained with what looked like black-berry juice. Her parasol was a bit ripped, where she had dragged it along hedges. One of her knicker-legs was drooping quite badly. Apart from that, she looked just the same.

Prudence and Solly stared at her. Then at each other. Then back to her again.

"I don't believe this," snarled Prudence. She marched up to the Prodigy, bent down, and shouted into her face. "Just what do you think you're doing?"

"Lookin' for Solly," said the Prodigy spiritedly.

"You see? What did I say?" Prudence glared at Solly, who was sheepishly scratching his head, wondering how he was to deal with this latest unexpected development. "Get rid of her. Now."

"Listen, Rosabella," said Solly. "This is ridiculous. You can't be more than five —"

"Six."

"All right, then, six. But you can't just up and run away like this, don't you see?"

"Why? I want to go to Town and get sweeties."

"Well, you're not coming with us," declared Prudence.

"I'll scweam," threatened the Prodigy. And opened her rosebud mouth to do so.

"Scream away," said Prudence with a shrug. "See if we care."

"No, don't!" begged Solly. "Whatever you do, *please* don't scream."

"All wight," agreed the Prodigy. "I won't, if *you* don't want me to, Solly. But I's still comin'."

"You're not sharing our food," snapped Prudence. "Is she, Solly?"

"Solly'll let me, won't you, Solly?" said the Prodigy, batting her lashes.

"No, he won't. Tell her, Solly," instructed Prudence, folding her bony arms and tapping her foot.

"Tell *her*," said the Prodigy with a sniff.

Both of them stood waiting. Solly tried out the beginnings of several sentences in his mind. None of them seemed to lead anywhere useful. Luckily, he was saved from having to respond because another sound met their ears. The sound of rumbling wheels, coming closer.

"A cart!" shouted Prudence, springing into action. "Quick! Flag it down!"

She sprinted across the grass and into the road just as the cart rounded the corner. It was empty, apart from a solitary bale of hay, and was pulled by a saggy old horse. The Carter was a sour-looking man in a wide-brimmed hat and stained smock. He was eating a large meat pie. He gave the reins a reluctant tug and stared down at Prudence with a look that wasn't promising.

"We need a lift," announced Prudence. "We're going to Town."

"Can't take yer there," growled the Carter. "I'm only going to Dullingham."

"But that's on the way, according to my map," said Prudence, taking it out and examining it. "Here. You see? Dullingham. About five miles ahead. You can take us to the turnoff."

"Oh, I can, can I?" said the Carter, chomping on his pie. It was clear he wasn't taking Prudence, who made things worse by saying, "Yes. You can," in her bossiest voice.

Solly and the Prodigy had been listening to this exchange with interest.

"Wait here, Solly," said the Prodigy. "She doesn't know how to do it."

She marched purposefully toward the cart. The Carter's gaze shifted away from Prudence and alighted on the Prodigy, who dropped a little curtsy. His eyes creased at the edges and his dour face took on a doting expression.

"Please, Mister Cart Man," said the Prodigy, doing the batting thing with her lashes. "Will you help us? Our sister's made us walk *so* far. My poor bwuvver's got sore feet, and I's *so* tired. I's only a lickle girl."

"Well now, little miss," said the Carter, completing his transformation into Father Christmas. " 'Ow can I refuse such a dear little face? 'Op on board. Want to sit up front with me? Mind you don't tear yer purty frock."

"Oh, fank you!" trilled the Prodigy, jumping up and down and clapping her hands. "Come on, Solly! He says we can!"

"You see?" said Solly as he climbed into the back with Prudence. "She's got her uses."

Prudence gave him a murderous look, and he said no more.

The cart was uncomfortable, but it was oh, such a relief to ride for a change. Solly stretched out his aching limbs and leaned his head against the hay, watching the dreary scenery go jolting past.

Up front, the Prodigy and the Carter were getting on like a house on fire. The Prodigy was prattling on about kittens and rainbows. The Carter kept saying he wished he had a little girl just like her and was giving her huge bites of his pie. The Prodigy was obviously having a fine time. At one point, she even burst into song. As far as they could make out, over the steady clip-clop of the horse's hooves, it was about a

Happy Land where lickle childwen played among the woses.

"Just look at her," fumed Prudence. "He's letting her hold the reins."

"Mmm," said Solly sleepily.

"I can't stand it. She puts it on, just like my sister Delight. She needs taking down a peg or two."

"Where the sun is shinin', where the birdies sing . . ."

"Did you hear me?"

"Mm."

"And lickle fishies swim awound beneaf the cwystal spwiiiiing . . ."

"We've got to get rid of her."

"We will," promised Solly. "We will, first opportunity."

"When?"

"When we get to Town. We'll hand her over to the magistrate."

"Even if she screams?"

"Even if she screams."

"Happy lickle childwen, playin' all day long . . ."

Prudence shuddered and stuffed hay in her ears.

It was beginning to get dark now and a thin, cold rain was beginning to fall. Up front, the Carter was wiping away a sentimental tear and looking for a blanket to tuck around the Prodigy's shoulders.

Solly pulled his threadbare jacket around him, hunkered down, and thought about his silver spoon. He hoped it would be worth it.

OOH!
I JUSS LOVE STORWIES!

⤙☙

In which Solly, Prudence, and the Prodigy

spend an uncomfortable night

and Prudence tells a secret.

Solly was having a dream. It was snowing. He was walking up the driveway of a huge house. He was walking fast, but never seemed to get any closer. In the distance, a sweeping stairway led up to enormous stone columns flanked with carved lions. Smooth white lawns spread out on either side. Trees hung heavy with snow.

Two figures stood beneath the columns. There was a tall man wearing a top hat and brandishing a huge silver spoon, which was as big as a garden spade. His face was in shadow. At his side stood a lady wearing a gray gown. Her face was veiled. For some reason, she had a large, flapping fish in her arms and was cradling it like a baby. It was a dream, so the fact that it was wearing a frilly bonnet didn't strike him as particularly odd.

As he approached, the man threw out his arms in welcoming fashion and was just about to step forward and reveal his face, when—

"Solly!" Hands were shaking him, none too gently.

"Mmf?"

"We've reached the turnoff. We're getting out."

"Groo?"

"Get out. This is as far as he goes."

It was really dark now, and still raining. Prudence was standing in the road, looking impatient. At the front of the cart, the Prodigy and the Carter were bidding each other a fond farewell. The Prodigy was hugging the Carter and kissing the horse. The Carter was insisting she keep the blanket. As a farewell gift, he presented her with a rosy red apple.

Solly shook his muzzy, dream-addled head and forced himself into action.

"You take good care of 'er, mind," the Carter told Solly and Prudence as he prepared to move off. "That's a little angel you got there. Too good fer this cruel world."

They stood and watched as he clicked to the horse and rumbled off into the night. The Prodigy waved and blew kisses until he was out of sight, then turned and said, with a triumphant leer, "See? *That's* how to do it."

"You think you're so good, don't you?" sneered Prudence.

"Yes," agreed the Prodigy. "I do."

"And that was supposed to be singing, was it? Is that your act? Singing sickly little songs to idiots who *pay*?"

"Yes. I's good at it. I got a blanket an' an apple. That's more'n you got."

"Oh, indeed? Well, let me tell you—"

"Prudence," broke in Solly. "Shouldn't we be looking for shelter? We can't stand here all night. We're getting soaked." He was scratching and yawning, desperate to get back to sleep.

The three of them stared around. They were in the middle of deserted countryside. The night was horribly black. There was no sound, apart from the rain dripping from leaves and the gleeful croaks of frogs in a nearby ditch. The wet, empty, miserable road stretched before them. It was no night to be out walking.

"What's that?" said Prudence, pointing to a dark, hulking shape a short way on.

"A barn, by the look of it," said Solly with a yawn, rubbing his bleary eyes.

"That'll do. Come on." And Prudence marched off.

The Prodigy took Solly's hand and said, "She's cwoss 'cause my nose is nicer."

"If I were you," advised Solly, trying to disengage her limpet grip, "I'd speak quieter."

The barn was little more than a ruin. A rusty plow leaned against the stone wall. The door hung by a single hinge. Beyond lay pitch-black darkness. They stood in the doorway, breathing in the heady scent of wet rot, dry rot, ancient manure, and damp, musty hay.

"Hold on," said Prudence. "I'll light the candle."

She scrabbled in her basket for the candle and matches. Shadows scurried away as the wick caught, and for the first time they were able to see their princely accommodation. The barn contained little other than a few abandoned tools, a log pile, an old barrel, some bales of hay, and a great many puddles where the roof was leaking. There were mice, too. Solly could hear rustling noises in the hay.

"It's cweepy," pronounced the Prodigy.

"It'll do," said Prudence.

"It's cweepy, isn't it, Solly?" insisted the Prodigy.

"Oh, well." Solly sighed. "At least it's drier than outside. You two make yourselves comfortable, and I'll prop the door up."

"Need any help?" offered Prudence.

"No, no. This is man's work."

He spat on his hands and manfully attempted to straighten the sagging door. After a minute or two of struggle, he stood back.

"There. That's bet—"

He hopped back hastily as it slowly keeled over. Rain blew in, on the back of a freezing wind.

Prudence gave a disparaging little snort and made herself at home in the choicest place on the hay bales. Having stuck her candle into a niche in the rough wall, she sat hunched over her composition book, scribbling. The Prodigy had gone for the barrel in the far corner. She had wrapped herself in the blanket and was greedily attacking the Carter's apple. Both had their backs to each other.

Solly hesitated. It was a tricky situation. Rival camps. Whichever one he sat next to, the other would take offense.

In the end, he decided to sit with his back to the log pile in between them, thus forming a perfect triangle.

A depressing silence fell. Prudence scribbled; the Prodigy munched. A mouse ran over Solly's foot. Rain coursed along the rotten beams and dripped into the puddles. It was very uncomfortable on the floor, leaning against logs. Exhausted though he was, sleep eluded him.

He turned on his left side, and a twig stabbed into his ear. He turned on his right, and a rusty nail gouged him in the neck. He lay on his back and thought about things. His spoon. Where he was going. Who he might turn out to be. Whether or not that would be better than who he was. Who would keep the water boiling while Ma did the daily wash. Things like that.

Still, he couldn't sleep.

"This is ridiculous," he said after a bit. His voice bounced around the rafters.

"What?" growled Prudence, scribbling like a mad thing.

"This—quarreling all the time. Whether we like it or not, we're stuck together at least until we get to Town. Why don't you both call a truce?"

"She started it," muttered Prudence.

"Di'n't," said the Prodigy.

"Yes, you did."

"Di'n't."

"Well, frankly, I think you're both as bad as each other," said Solly. "Prudence, you're cross all the time."

"No I'm not," said Prudence crossly.

"Yes, you are. Most of the time, anyway."

"You are," said the Prodigy with a nod.

"And you, Rosabella—you're greedy," added Solly, just to be fair.

"Not," said the Prodigy, eating her apple.

"What about you, then, Solly?" snapped Prudence. "You're not exactly perfect yourself. I thought you were a bit different from other boys, but I can see now that I was just deceived by your napkin. You're just as—"

"WAAAAAAAAAAAAAAH!" The Prodigy let out a sudden, shrill, earsplitting screech. There came a scrabble of panicky footsteps. Solly sat bolt upright, heart pounding. Prudence was screaming as well. Both girls were standing on the hay bales, clutching onto each other and pointing.

"A wat!" shrieked the Prodigy.

"There!" bellowed Prudence. "It is! A rat!"

"It's a mouse," said Solly.

"It's a wat!"

"It's a *mouse*. A tiny little harvest one. I know because it ran over my foot."

"There it is, look!" Prudence was dancing around, clutching at her skirt. "She's right! It's a—oh. Solly's right. It's a mouse. Quite a sweet one, actually."

"Oh," said the Prodigy. "Where?"

"It's gone now."

Rather sheepishly, they both sat down.

"Honestly," scoffed Solly. "Fancy being scared of a little mouse."

"Shut up," they both chorused.

"Just because he was born with a silver spoon in his mouth, he thinks he can say anything," said Prudence to the Prodigy.

"Were you weally, Solly?" asked the Prodigy, arranging her blanket across her lap.

"Well, I don't know that I was *born* with it in my mouth," said Solly. "It was in the basket I came in, though."

"He's a foundling," explained Prudence. "Left on a doorstep. Raised as a washer boy. Parents pawned the spoon. He's only just found out. Now he's off to track it down and find out if he's a lord and claim his inheritance. Right?"

"More or less," said Solly, miffed that his fascinating story could be told in so few words.

"I know a storwy 'bout a boy lord," the Prodigy told Prudence. "It's called *Lickle Lord Forklewoy*. I 'speck Solly'll be *Lickle Lord Spoonlewoy*."

Both of them sniggered.

"Do you want my apple core, Pwudence?" offered the Prodigy.

"All right," said Prudence, quite pleasantly for once. "Thanks."

Honestly, thought Solly. Girls. He'd never get to understand girls if he lived to be twenty.

"What you doin', Pwudence?" asked the Prodigy. She peered at the composition book, which had fallen into the hay, along with the pencil.

"Writing," said Prudence. "Except I've lost my pencil."

"Here it is. I founded it for you."

"Oh. Thanks."

"What you witin'?"

"Just notes," mumbled Prudence. "For a story I'm writing."

Solly's ears pricked up. She was writing a story? This was the first he'd heard about it.

"Ooh!" squealed the Prodigy, clapping her hands. "I juss love storwies! I know one 'bout a lickle wabbit called Wodger who—"

"Rosabella," interrupted Prudence, "just stop, all right?"

"Stop what, Pwudence?"

"Your act. All the stuff about 'lickle wabbits.' And the babyish handclapping and that thing you do with your eyes. It might impress other people, but it doesn't wash with me."

"All wight," said the Prodigy meekly. "Sowwy."

"And while you're at it, talk properly. It's 'rabbit.' Not 'wabbit.'"

"All wight. I'll twy. What's your storwy called?"

Prudence looked up and caught Solly's eye. She looked a bit sheepish, and the tip of her nose was turning red. Suddenly, it all fell into place.

"I think I know," said Solly. "It's called *Little Sir Thummagain.* The one about Bugless Scum and the embroidered hankie. You didn't read it at all. You wrote it. Didn't you?"

"Um, yes," admitted Prudence. "What about it?"

"Nothing. It's good. And you wrote it all on your own?"

"Yes."

"With no help? It just came out of your brain?"

"Yes. Well, I haven't finished writing it yet. It's a work in progress. But the publishers only need to see the first few pages to know if it's good or not."

"What's a pubble chair?" the Prodigy wanted to know.

"They make books," explained Prudence. "People write stories, then the publishers print them up, with your name on them and everything. They give you money for it."

"Will they pwint *Lickle Sir Thummagain*?"

"I don't know. Maybe. That's why I'm going to Town."

Aha! thought Solly. So that's why.

"Why the big secret?" he asked. "Why didn't you tell me before?"

"I don't know." Prudence shrugged. "I suppose I didn't want you to laugh."

"Why would I laugh?" Solly was genuinely astonished.

"Most people do. Poachers' daughters aren't

known for their novels. Well, Dad's quite encouraging, being a bit of a rebel himself, but he's in jail again. Ma just thinks I'm crazy. She says girls can't be writers and I'm wasting my time."

"Well, take no notice," said Solly stoutly. "They're just jealous. It's a good story."

"Really?" Prudence looked pleased. "Well, let's hope the publishers agree and give me some money. We could certainly do with it."

"What's the storwy about?" asked the Prodigy. She gave a huge yawn, stuck her thumb in her mouth, and leaned against Prudence.

"Bugless Scum. He's a foundling."

"Like Solly."

"No. Not a bit. Taller and more handsome. And stronger. And braver. Doesn't moan. With curly hair."

"She means he's a proper hero," explained Solly. "When Bugless fixes doors, they stay fixed. Right, Prudence?"

"Wead some," said the Prodigy.

"I don't usually like to read things until I've finished," hedged Prudence.

"Go on," urged Solly. He stood up and stretched

his aching limbs. "We won't laugh. Read us a bit. I'm coming to join you, if you don't mind. I'm sure Bugless wouldn't mind sitting in a draft, but I'm freezing."

Both girls made room for him on the hay bale. The Prodigy, generous for once, spread the Carter's blanket over their knees. It wasn't exactly cozy, but it was a good deal better than the floor.

"Ready?" said Prudence. "Then I'll begin."

And she began to read.

"'There once lived, in the county of Devonshire, a gentleman of tall stature and noble features called Lord Royston Thummagain. He always wore top hats and well-cut trousers and carried a gold watch in his waistcoat pocket. He dined on venison and sipped wine from crystal glasses. Everyone liked him because he was kind to the poor and never, ever threw poachers in jail.

"'The noble lord would have been quite content if only he had a wife, but none of the fine ladies he knew were quite right for him.'"

"Like the pwince in Cindewella," murmured the Prodigy dreamily.

"When do we get to Bugless?" asked Solly.

"Shush. All in good time. 'One day, when out

riding Midnight, his black stallion, Lord Royston met his perfect match. Her name was Lady Tatania Scone and she was dangling by her luxurious hair from a ravine because she had fallen off her horse, called Merrilegs. She wore a beautiful green velvet riding habit and a matching hat and fashionable boots. Diamond earrings glistened in her dainty ears—'"

"There's a lot about what people are wearing," remarked Solly.

"Do you want to hear this or don't you?"

"Yes."

"And who's writing this story, anyway?"

"Sorry, sorry. Do go on."

"I *like* the clothes," said the Prodigy sleepily. She snuggled against Solly. "I like the lady's widing fings."

"'"Help," cried the poor lady. "Save me, Lord Thummagain." "Call me Royston," said the brave lord, and he rescued her, at great risk to himself. So they got married the next day.'"

"What—just like that?" objected Solly.

"Yes. Why not?"

"Well, they hardly know each other. She probably picks her feet in bed. He could have a gambling habit or—or dandruff or something. When do we get to Bugless?"

"Later. 'For the wedding, Lord Royston wore his best suit, and Lady Tatania wore a wonderful bridal gown. It was all white, with lace ruffles, and trimmed with rosebuds. On her feet, she wore—'"

At that point, the candle guttered out and Prudence was forced to stop. Solly couldn't say he was that sorry. Privately, he felt that the clothes were slowing up the action. And Bugless wasn't even born yet. There were a lot of good words, though. Prudence certainly knew how to write.

He lay back on the hay, closed his eyes, and thought about his silver spoon. Then he tried to imagine what his real parents might be like. He couldn't get beyond tall hat and gray dress, so he gave up.

He wondered how Ma and Pa were getting on without him. He hoped they were coping.

He pushed away the Prodigy, who was slumped heavily on his shoulder. Prudence was snoring lightly. The rain dripped.

He hauled on the blanket, turned over, and drifted away. This time, he had no dreams.

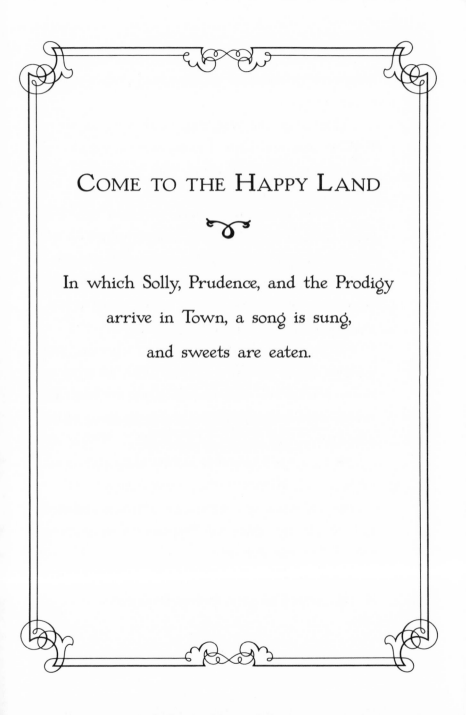

COME TO THE HAPPY LAND

In which Solly, Prudence, and the Prodigy

arrive in Town, a song is sung,

and sweets are eaten.

Town! Town, at last!

What a contrast to the country. Coaches, carriages, cabs, donkey carts, and wagons choked the cobbled streets. Light spilled from the bulging windows of shops, with a thousand and one goods on show — shoes, hats, bread, medicines. Solly had never dreamed that there was so much to buy in the world.

And the people! Women with baskets on their heads, milkmaids carrying pails, men bent double under whole carcasses of meat, fine ladies in stiff, wide dresses and top-hatted gentlemen strolling in and out of shops, hawkers of ribbons, knife grinders, match sellers, beggars, urchins, thieves, and idlers all mingled together in a pushing, shouting, heaving mass. The air was thick with pungent smoke, which belched from every chimney.

"I don't believe this!" gasped Solly. "It's so —" He waved his hands around, searching for the right word.

"Noisy?" said Prudence. "Smelly? Busy? *Rude?*" She glared at a passerby who had just trodden on her foot.

"All of that," agreed Solly. "And gas lamps, too. I've never seen those before." He pointed to the nearest lamppost, where a group of disreputable-looking youths was lounging around.

It was late afternoon. The rain had stopped, but it was still bitterly cold. Travel-stained, weary, and still aching after their night in the barn, they had finally reached Town on a wagon laden with potatoes—the third ride of the day. The other two had been with a whiskery old man on a donkey cart and a gruff farmer on a haywain. The Prodigy had proved unfailingly talented at securing rides. One bat of her lashes was all it took. Every time, Prudence made a face and muttered under her breath. Her disapproval of the Prodigy's methods didn't stop her from getting in, though, Solly noticed.

Right now, the three of them stood outside a pie shop, backs pressed to the wall as the townsfolk shoved and elbowed their way past. The tantalizing smell of warm pastry drifted from the shop. Solly was almost drooling. He would die if he didn't eat soon.

"Any bread left?" he asked, not very hopefully.

"No," said Prudence. "All gone. We ate the last of it hours ago."

"Could we buy a pie?"

"They're a penny each," said Prudence. "Three of those and that's half my life savings gone out the window. I didn't think things would be so expensive."

"I want sweeties," said the Prodigy.

"Well, you can't have any," snapped Prudence. The Prodigy had scored high in the eating stakes as well. She always ended up in front, next to the driver. Altogether, she had netted a meat pie, an apple, two carrots, a thick slice of raisin bread, and a juicy pear, all of which she had selfishly eaten herself.

"Why not?"

"Because you haven't got any money, have you?"

"No," admitted the Prodigy. "But that's easy. I can get some."

"Oh yes? How?"

"Like this."

The Prodigy took her blanket off her shoulders and handed both it and her little blue parasol to Prudence. She stood on tiptoe and removed Solly's cap. She then stepped boldly into the path of the bustling hordes and placed the cap on the cobbles. She smoothed down her crumpled blue dress. Then she pointed a toe, clasped her hands together, put on a soulful look, and, to Prudence and Solly's horror, began to sing.

"Come to the Happy Land and play among the woses. Here in the Happy Land, nothin' can go wong. . . ."

"Stop her!" hissed Prudence.

"You stop her," muttered Solly. "I'm not having anything to do with it."

"See the little wabbits hoppin' in the cornfields . . ."

"But she's singing for sweets money! That's degrading!"

"Lickle wobin wedbweast warblin' his song. . . ."

Amazingly, people were stopping to look and listen. A milkmaid had set down her pail and was wiping away a tear with the hem of her apron. A stout matron stopped in her tracks, hesitated, then rummaged for her purse. An elderly gentleman in a frock coat ground to a halt, cocked an ear, then took out a handkerchief and blew his nose. The gang of disreputable youths under the lamppost fell silent and moved in closer. Solly found their interest a little odd. They didn't look like music lovers.

"Wound and wound the garden, pickin' pwetty flowers . . ."

"I can't take this," grumbled Prudence. "It's the most disgusting display I've ever seen."

"Wows of wowdedendwums, gwowing wild and fweeee. . . ."

"But they're giving her money!" Solly pointed out.

They were, too. Solly couldn't see the Prodigy now—the crowd around her was too thick. But there came the distinct sound of coins clinking into the cap.

"Come to the Happy Land and play among the woses . . ."

"I'm putting a stop to this," announced Prudence.

"But she's just doing what she does. You'd like some sweets, wouldn't you? We need money, don't we? You're so keen to hang on to your old sixpence."

He regretted saying that the moment it left his lips. Prudence gave him a hurt glance.

"Sorry," he amended. "I didn't mean that. I know it's yours."

"I'm just trying to be prudent, that's all. Anyway, we shouldn't get money like this. It's no better than begging. Worse. Even beggars don't show off. If you won't get her, I will."

Grimly, she plunged into the throng. Solly stayed right where he was. This was rich. The poacher's daughter getting all self-righteous about taking something for nothing.

"Here in the Happy Land, that's the place to beeeeeee!"

The appalling song ended on a high, wobbly note, which the Prodigy hung on to for dear life. When she finally ran out of breath, there was a storm of enthusiastic clapping and loud cries for more.

Suddenly, the cheers turned to low muttering and a few boos. The crowd parted as Prudence came marching through with a face like thunder, dragging the Prodigy behind her.

"Don't you ever, ever show us up like that again!" scolded Prudence. The Prodigy's disappointed fans were slowly dispersing, giving Prudence black looks. "That was so embarrassing. Tell her, Solly."

"How much did you get?" Solly asked the Prodigy, avoiding Prudence's eyes.

The Prodigy looked in the cap. "Two pennies, three ha'pennies, four farthin's, an' a button."

"How many sweets will that buy?"

"Lots."

"Then what are we waiting for? Let's go."

"Traitor!" hissed Prudence.

A short while later, Solly and Prudence stood in a side street, watching the Prodigy debase herself for sweets. There had been a market earlier that day. The traders were busy taking down their stalls and packing away their wares.

The Prodigy had spotted a seller of lurid confectionery loading the last of his unsold stock onto a hand cart. He was anxious to home. It was highly inconvenient to get them out again, but he had reckoned without the Prodigy's considerable powers of persuasion.

"I wonder what they'll taste like," said Solly. His mouth was already watering with anticipation. "I've never had a sweet. All we ever have at home is pottage. Have you ever had a sweet?"

Prudence wasn't speaking.

"Oh, come on," said Solly, eyes fixed on the distant blue bonnet. "You know you want to. Admit it."

Prudence folded her arms and said, "When are we taking her to the magistrate?"

"What?"

"You said we'd dump her at the magistrate's."

"I know," said Solly. The Prodigy and the sweetseller had reached the end of their transaction. The Prodigy was approaching with a large, knobbly-looking paper bag.

"So when, then?"

"I don't know. Soon. Did you get some?" This last sentence was addressed to the Prodigy, whose mouth was already bulging.

"Yes. I got acid dwops an' pear dwops an' jelly babies an' barley sugar an' liquowice an' aniseed balls an' humbugs. Have one." She proffered the bag.

Solly's knees went weak. He stared down at the ravishing selection. He had dreamed of this moment, especially on Turnip Sundays.

"Take a gween one," suggested the Prodigy.

Solly took a green one. He placed it on his tongue, slowly withdrew his tongue into his mouth, and gave an experimental suck.

Oh, rapture! Bells! Flights of skylarks! Rainbows! Explosions of fireworks! Could there be such an exquisite, marvelous, utterly delectable taste?

It was, without doubt, the best moment in his life so far. He closed his eyes and sucked away with gusto.

"He gave me lots of bwoke ones fwee," said the Prodigy, crunching away. "'Cause I's pwett—" She caught sight of Prudence's face, abruptly changed her mind, and said, quite politely, "Do you want one, Pwudence?"

"You see?" said Solly, sucking away happily. "She's getting better. At least she's learning to share. That was very nice of you, Rosabella. Go on, Prudence—they're lovely."

"Take a gween one," encouraged the Prodigy.

Prudence stared at both of them, then the bag. She was obviously going through an intense inner struggle. Finally, temptation got the better of her and she said snappishly, "I'll take a red one," and did so.

"To match your nose," said the Prodigy innocently. Prudence gave her a look.

"Now what?" said Solly.

He looked up the narrow street, which was rapidly emptying. Piles of rubbish were strewn about. A stray dog was nosing about among cabbage stalks and bruised apples. A rough-looking man—a butcher, by the look of him—was loading a dead pig and crates full of live chickens onto a pony cart, which was waiting around the corner. It was getting dark. Colder, too.

Solly stamped his feet, blew on his hands, and finished his green sweet in three satisfying crunches. He looked hopefully at the bag, and the Prodigy gave him another one.

"Now we look for your pawnshop," said Prudence, helping herself to a humbug.

"I hate pwawns," the Prodigy informed them, through a mouthful of jelly baby. "Pink slugs— yucky."

"What about your publisher?" asked Solly.

"That can wait until the morning. They'll be closed now. But pawnshops stay open late. That's when they do the most business. People get more desperate at night. That's when they sell their wedding rings and their granny's brooches. You can't eat gold."

"True." Solly nodded, thinking that Prudence could be very profound at times. Probably because she was a writer.

Behind them, the butcher disappeared around the corner, leaving a single, solitary crate. Mouth crammed with sugar, the Prodigy wandered over to take a look at it. She crouched down and peered in.

"Ooooh!" she squealed, beckoning urgently. "Come an' look! A wabbit! A dear lickle bunny wabbit wiv floppy ears!"

It was, too. In the bottom of the crate was a small brown rabbit with ears that drooped like the leaves on a rain-starved banana tree. It twitched its nose once, then just sat there, looking stupid. The Prodigy pressed her ear to the crate, listened, and said, "He says he doesn't like it in there."

"I'm not surprised, poor thing," said Solly. The crate was a very small one. Not that the rabbit seemed to care much. It didn't look as if it had a brain in its head.

"Destined for the pot tomorrow, I expect," said Prudence, the poacher's daughter. The Prodigy gave a wail and clutched at Solly's knees.

"Oh, noooooo!"

"There, there," said Solly with a warning glance at Prudence. "Somebody'll have a lovely hot supper. Think of it like that."

"I love rabbit stew," said Prudence. "Yum, yum. More gravy, please."

"But I don't want him eated!" protested the Prodigy.

"Yum, yum," repeated Prudence, rubbing her tummy.

"But we can wescue him! 'Fore the man gets back! 'Fore he gets deaded!"

"Yum, yum," said Prudence, licking her lips, enjoying herself.

"Solly!" cried the Prodigy, eyes brimming over. "Tell her!"

"Come on," said Solly. He hauled the Prodigy to her feet. "We can't do anything about it."

"And don't even think about screaming," warned Prudence. "Or we'll leave you here all on your own."

"I wasn't," said the Prodigy with a sniff, wiping her nose with her blanket. Firmly, Solly took her hand and, feeling a bit rotten, began towing her up the street.

"The sign with three balls," said Prudence briskly as they reached the end and turned the corner. "That's what we're looking for. It's sure to be around here somewhere. We could try up there." She pointed up a dark, rubbish-strewn alleyway leading between the backs of houses. "That looks likely."

"Why that one? There are alleyways everywhere,"

said Solly, gazing around. The back streets were a maze. Away from the main street, the gas lamps were few and far between. Looking for one particular shop wasn't going to be easy. It was getting colder by the minute, too. His teeth were chattering. Only one thing could take his mind off things.

"Can I have another sweet, Rosabella?"

"Ooops!" The Prodigy's eyes widened. She clapped a hand to her rosebud mouth. "Silly me! I lefted 'em behind!"

"*What?* You left the *sweets* behind?" Solly was aghast. He really had a craving.

"Wait, I'll get 'em!"

Before he could stop her, she went racing back the way they had come, little boots tippy-tapping and blanket trailing in the dirt.

"We have to start somewhere," said Prudence, stopping in the dim yellow light of a solitary streetlamp. "I'll go up it a little way. You wait here for Rosabella. Don't let her eat any more until I get back."

"But suppose you get attacked? It's really dark up there."

"I'll rattle my crow-scarer and whack 'em with my basket and you can come to my aid."

"I still think I should go. I bet Bugless would."

"Well, yes. But you're better with Rosabella, so stay here."

So saying, she marched off, leaving Solly hovering on the corner under the lamp. He waited until she was swallowed by the shadows, then stamped his feet and shivered as the sharp wind blew through his jacket. He looked up at the sliver of sky. The stars were low. It looked like frost. He blew on his fingers, then peered anxiously back down the street, hoping the Prodigy wouldn't be long. His mouth was watering already.

Somewhere in the distance, a clock struck ten.

A rat shot from a pile of rubbish, making him jump.

He thought he heard a muffled cough coming from one of the alleys, but when he looked, there was no one there.

Finally, the welcome sound of tippy-tapping announced the triumphant return of the Prodigy. She came trotting up the street clutching—thank you, thank you!—the bag of sweets. At the same time, Prudence emerged from the alleyway, looking very pleased with herself.

"It's up there," she announced. "Told you. The

sign with the three balls, just like I said. It's still open, too."

"An' I got the sweeties," said the Prodigy, pulling her blanket around her and holding out the bag.

"Great!" enthused Solly, helping himself to a humbug.

Things were looking up.

PERFECT PARENTS
INTERLUDE THREE

In which Lady Elvira and
Lord Charles have dinner and
make plans for a social gathering.

"Delicious pheasant, my dear," remarked Lord Charles. They sat at either end of a long table in the dining room. A massive chandelier hung overhead. Family portraits adorned the walls. "Are you not hungry this evening?"

"No," sighed Lady Elvira. "Somehow, I haven't the heart to eat. Not knowing whether or not our precious boy is enjoying his supper."

"Now, come along, darling. You're not helping him by not eating, are you?"

"I suppose not. But, oh, Charles! His birthday is coming up! How can I eat, drink, and be merry? A mother's love knows no bounds."

"There, there," soothed her husband. "Calm yourself. Look, why not throw a little dinner party? It will take your mind off things. You could invite the Channingpot Crisplys and the Chumpingtons. And maybe the Heyho sisters. They're lively. And I could invite old Tumpty Tweezle from the club."

"Lord Tweezle? I thought he was hunting big game in foreign parts."

"Came back. Living in Town. Taking a keen interest in parish affairs, I hear. Sitting on various boards and so on. Says they haven't a clue how to manage money. Tumpty'll sort 'em out—you can be sure of it. What do you say?"

"Oh, Charles. I'm not sure I'm up to it."

"Oh, come on, darling. It'll be a jolly evening. You could wear your new blue gown. The ladies can sing around the piano and play charades while we men smoke cigars over a game of poker."

"Very well, dearest," agreed her Ladyship quietly. "If you think it best. But I fear I shall be dull company."

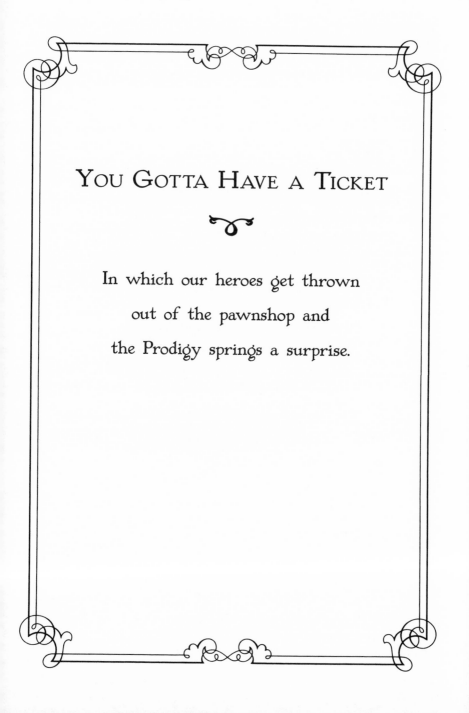

You Gotta Have a Ticket

In which our heroes get thrown
out of the pawnshop and
the Prodigy springs a surprise.

Y es?" said the man behind the counter. His fishy eyes swam down at them through a pair of wire-rimmed spectacles. He wore half-fingered gloves and a rusty black frock coat. His lank gray hair hung like greasy curtains on either side of his cadaverous face.

Prudence gave Solly a dig in the ribs.

"Told you," she muttered. "Fingerless gloves."

"Um, excuse me, sir," said Solly. "I'm wondering if you can help me."

"I doubt it," said the man with an unpleasant smirk. "Unless you've got your dear old granny's diamonds among them rags."

He was bent over a small set of scales, on which was balanced a plain gold wedding band. Beneath the glass counter was a display of tawdry jewelery. Cheap rings, broken necklaces, bracelets, and brooches were laid out, together with scratched cigar cases, ancient watches, and tin snuffboxes. Each had a yellowing label attached.

More of the same was exhibited in tall, dark glass-fronted cases around the shop. There was other stuff, too. Boxes of old tin cutlery. Ugly china ornaments, thick with the dust of ages. A stuffed fox. A rusty parrot cage. A bugle. Shelves of moldering books. A violin with no strings. Cases of pinned butterflies. A folding screen, covered with glued-on paper cutouts of sailor-suited boys and small, frilly girls. A sad pair of faded, pink, down-at-heel dancing shoes. Stopped clocks. Chipped crockery. There was no end to the junk.

The Prodigy, well muffled in her blanket, wandered around, sucking noisily on a mouthful of aniseed balls.

"Don't you touch nothing, mind!" said the pawnbroker.

"I wasn't," protested the Prodigy.

"So you say."

"No, weally I wasn't." The Prodigy batted her lashes. "Shall I sing you a song 'bout an angel, Mister Pwawn Man?"

"No. Keep your sticky little paws to yourself, you hear?"

Amazingly, it seemed that the pawnbroker was immune to the Prodigy's charms.

"Ahem." Solly gave a little cough, and the fishy eyes swam back to him. "Look. I'm sorry to bother you, but I just wanted to make some inquiries about a spoon."

"I got a lot o' spoons."

"No, no. I don't want just any old spoon. This one's special. My pa brought it in. Sometime last November."

"Got the ticket?"

"Er, no."

"How d'you expect me to find it, then? You gotta have a ticket."

"Couldn't you look it up?" suggested Prudence. She pointed past him, to a shelf stuffed with old ledgers. "You must have a record of your transactions."

"Oh, I must, must I?"

"Yes. His pa's called Scubbins. Do you keep your books in date order, or alphabetically?"

"None o' your concern how I does it," said the pawnbroker. "Oi! What did I just say?"

The Prodigy was surreptitiously trying to peel a frilly girl from the screen. She stopped and pouted a bit.

"I'd be ever so grateful," said Solly. "It's important. This is a really special spoon. It's a family heir-loom. I think it might have letters engraved on it."

"What letters?"

"I don't know," admitted poor Solly.

The pawnbroker gave a shrug. "Out of luck, then, aren't you?"

"Look," said Prudence. "It's not too much to ask, is it? We just need to know whether or not you've still got it. You should have. You're sup-posed to keep it for a year."

"And *you're* supposed to have a ticket," shot back the pawnbroker. Stalemate.

"So have you got it?" demanded Prudence. "That's all we want to know."

"What if I have?"

"Then we'll buy it off you."

"Oh, you will, will you? And how much have you got?"

"Sixpence," said Prudence.

Solly stared at her, mouth open. She was pre-pared to hand over her entire life savings, just like that! And to think he had accused her of being mean.

"Sixpence won't do," sneered the pawnbroker. "Not if it's real silver. If it's any good, I'll have sold it anyway, so you're wasting your time."

"Well, if you'll just tell us who bought it, we can track it down, can't we?" Prudence had a real edge to her voice.

"Well, you *could* . . ." agreed the pawnbroker, every bit as steely.

"There you go, then!"

"If I could be bothered to look it up," finished the pawnbroker with a triumphant leer. "Which I can't."

"Well!" snapped Prudence. "You really are the most unhelpful man I have ever met."

"That's me," agreed the pawnbroker. "Now, if you'll kindly take your beaky nose out of here, missy, I'll get on with my work."

"Leave her nose out of it," said Solly.

"And don't you be cheeky neither," said the pawnbroker. "I've a mind to call out the night watch and you can all spend the night in a cell."

"Come on, Solly," said Prudence. "We're wasting time. Let's go."

She grabbed his arm and pulled him toward the door, then paused for her parting shot.

"Tell me," she said. "Your name's not Zebediah Stinge, by any chance, is it?"

"No," growled the pawnbroker. "It's Lazarus Pinchpenny. What of it?"

"Hah!" Prudence gave a short, hard laugh. "See what I mean, Solly?"

"I most certainly do," agreed Solly.

And with that, they stalked out of the shop, pausing only to collect the Prodigy, who was ramming the tip of her parasol into the hole in a cuckoo clock, attempting to pry out its occupant.

Outside, the cold hit them like a knife. Frost glittered on the cobbles as they moved away from the shop, some way down the alley. Stars scattered the sky, casting a romantic silver glow on a nearby heap of broken furniture and household rubbish, which was piled high against the wall. They stood in a miserable huddle, debating what to do next.

"Well, that didn't go according to plan," said Solly through chattering teeth.

"I didn't expect it to," said Prudence. "Told you, didn't I? Horrible old man."

"Wasn't he?" agreed Solly. "It can't be that difficult to look up who bought my spoon. Unless he's got it and isn't telling us out of spite."

"Of course he hasn't got it. He's sold it. Didn't you see how shifty he looked?"

"So what do you think we should do?"

"I don't know. I'm thinking." Absently,

Prudence removed her pencil from her bonnet and began scratching her nose.

"What would Bugless do in a situation like this?"

"Ah." Prudence sounded more confident. "He'd wait around until the pawnbroker locked up and went home for the night. Then he'd break in and look it up himself in the ledger—Rosabella! Are you eating the last of the sweets?"

"No," said the Prodigy. She had moved away from them and was standing with her back turned, fiddling with something.

"How many left?"

"Some."

"Hand them over, then."

"Juss a minute."

"What are you huddled up like that for? Are you hiding something under that blanket?"

"No."

"I don't believe you. You took something from the shop, didn't you?"

Prudence made a dive. The Prodigy tried to elude her. Several items fell out of her knicker-legs and sprayed all over the cobbles. A chipped china sheep. A pink dancing slipper. A small, cast-iron shovel. A paper cut-out frilly girl.

"Rosabella!" Solly gasped. "You are such a thief!"

"She's got something else under there!" shouted Prudence. "Get her!"

Solly made a grab. The Prodigy hopped to one side, but in doing so, she tripped over the hem of her blanket. It fell to the icy ground. And there, cradled in her arms, staring blankly straight ahead was—

"The rabbit!" groaned Solly. "She's only gone and taken the flippin' rabbit!"

"You stupid girl!" raged Prudence. "I might have known you'd do something like that!"

"He's mine!" wailed the Prodigy. "I wescued him an' he's mine!"

"Give," demanded Prudence, holding her arms out.

"No!" The Prodigy backed away.

"Give me that rabbit!"

"I won't. I love him."

"Leave this to me," sighed Solly. He took a step forward. The Prodigy took another step back, quivering like a stag at bay. Solly crouched down.

"Look, Rosabella," he said gently. "You can't keep a rabbit."

"Why not?"

"Because rabbits need to live in a nice, warm hutch."

"He says he hasn't got a hutch. He says all he's got is a howwid old cwate!"

The Prodigy's eyes were filling with tears. She clutched fiercely onto the rabbit, who looked uninterested.

"Besides," continued Solly, "rabbits need special things to eat. Lettuce and — stuff."

"He's got lettuce," pleaded the Prodigy, pointing at a huge sack of vegetable waste spilling into the road. "He can live under my blanket. I can feed him. I can! I can!"

"Too much lettuce gives rabbits gas," chipped in Prudence.

"What do you care!" The Prodigy glared through her tears. "You wanted him for your *dinner*!" She stamped her little foot.

"Anyway," Solly went on patiently, "you can't carry it around forever. You'll have to put it down sometimes, because it'll need to — you know. Do its business."

"So?"

"So it'll hop away first chance it gets."

"No, he won't. He loves me. He said so."

"Try it," sneered Prudence. "Put it down. See what it does."

"Don't say 'it.' He's a *him*."

"All right, then, him. Put him down and see what he does."

The Prodigy hesitated a moment. Then, carefully, she bent down and placed the rabbit on the freezing cobbles. It just sat there.

All three of them watched it.

"Fascinating," said Prudence. "Do you think he knows any other tricks?"

Solly nudged it gently with his foot. The rabbit allowed itself to be pushed.

"Cold, I 'spect," said the Prodigy.

"Thick," said Prudence. "Thick as a plank. That's all we need, a thick rabbit. You're not keeping him, Rosabella. Rabbits don't belong on serious quests."

"It doesn't even hop," said Solly. "I thought all rabbits hopped. It's more like a vegetable than a rabbit. Why doesn't it do something?" The Prodigy glared reproachfully. "Sorry, I mean he."

"I've seen turnips with more animation," agreed Prudence.

"You see?" said the Prodigy. "He doesn't want to leave me."

She bent down and scooped the unresponsive rabbit into her arms. Just in time, too, because at that very moment, there came the sound of a banging door.

Together, the three of them scurried behind the rubbish heap and crouched down, trying not to breathe.

Back up the alley, the pawnbroker emerged from his shop. He stood muttering to himself as he fussed with shutters and fiddled with a large bunch of keys. His breath came in little puffs as he breathed the frosty air. Finally he got the door locked to his satisfaction. Then he placed a tall hat on his head and set off in the other direction.

"Right!" said Prudence grimly as soon as the echoing footsteps had died away. "Time for a bit of breaking and entering."

OOSHTUG!

❧

In which the rabbit is named,
Solly's lips are sealed, and a
new acquaintance introduces himself
to the Intelligent Reader.

Lazarus Pinchpenny obviously didn't believe in taking chances. His shop was better protected than a bank vault. Shutters were securely pulled down over the leaded windows, and the stout door was firmly locked.

"It's hopeless," sighed Solly after examining it from every possible angle. "We'll never get in. We'd need a battering ram. And even then, the street's too narrow to get a proper run at the door. Cripes, it's freezing out here." He stamped his feet to get the circulation going.

"What about that high window up there, just below the roof?" suggested Prudence. The cold was turning the tip of her nose an unpleasant shade of blue. "We could try standing on each other's shoulders."

"We still wouldn't reach. And it's sure to be locked and bolted anyway."

"Hey, look!" said Prudence. "There's a long pole here. It's got a brush on the end. Probably left by a chimney sweep. Can't we do something with that?"

"Like what?" scoffed Solly. "How's a long thin pole with a brush on the end going to help? This shop's a fortress."

"Even so."

"Prudence, it's a pole. It's long. It's thin. It's got a brush on the end. It's about as much use as — as your pencil. Don't talk so daft."

"Bugless would think of something," said Prudence tightly. The tip of her nose was turning — purple. She didn't appreciate his casual dismissal of the brush.

"Oh, right. Bugless. Of course, *Bugless* would."

"Well, he would."

"Like what?" sneered Solly. He knew he was being unpleasant, but what with the disappointment about the spoon plus the stupid rabbit and the cold and everything, he just couldn't help it. Having Bugless thrown in his face was the final straw.

"Like, I don't know yet. I'm thinking."

"Well, if you can make Bugless come up with an idea of how to break into a fortress using a long thin pole with a brush on the end, I'd very much like to hear it."

"Shut up."

"Next, you'll be suggesting we can do something with your crow-scarer."

"I said *shut up*."

"All right."

A silence fell. Prudence gnawed on her pencil. Solly folded his arms and waited, pointedly tapping his foot.

"Are you two goin' to be much longer arguwin'?" asked the Prodigy.

"Shut up!" snarled Solly and Prudence together.

"All wight," agreed the Prodigy.

There was another pause. Then, "Sorry," said Solly. He reached out and patted Prudence's bony shoulder. "I didn't mean to be rotten. I'm just so—" He waved his hands around. "You know. What's the right word? When you shout at people because nothing's going right?"

"Frustrated," supplied Prudence with a sigh. "I know. Me, too."

They stared helplessly at the impregnable shop.

"I know how you can get in," said the Prodigy.

She was sitting on the curb, cradling the rabbit. Its indifferent head stuck up over the blanket. It showed no signs of cold, pleasure, fear, affection, irritation, or anything at all, really.

"Don't be silly," said Prudence.

"I do so."

"How?" asked Solly. He felt a sudden surge of hope. She was a circus girl, after all. Circus people had certain skills, didn't they? Maybe she could pick locks. Or she might have some ingenious plan involving ropes or acrobatics or some such athletic thing. Even the sweep's brush, although he sort of hoped not.

"I's not tellin'. 'Less I can keep Mr. Skippy."

"'Mr. Skippy'?" chorused Solly and Prudence. They stared incredulously at each other, then down at the turgid lump in the Prodigy's arms.

"That's a *dog's* name," said Prudence. "A frisky little puppy dog. Not some brainless cabbage head that just sits."

"Well, that's his name," said the Prodigy firmly. She kissed his furry ears.

"Could be worse," Solly told Prudence. "Could be 'Wodger.'"

"How do you know it's a he, anyway?" asked Prudence.

The Prodigy looked scornful. " 'Cause girl wabbits aren't called Mr. Skippy."

There was no answer to that.

"All right," agreed Solly. "Tell us how to do it. If it works, you can keep him."

"Weally?" The Prodigy's face lit up. "I can?"

"Yes," said Solly, firmly avoiding looking at Prudence. "You can. So, how do we get in?"

"Wiv this," said the Prodigy. And she took a big brass key from her knicker-leg and held it out.

"What?" gasped Solly, flabbergasted. "You've got the key? But—how?"

"I tooked it off the hook. When you was talkin' to the pwawn man. It was nex' to the door. It said 'spare key' on the label. It's not juss Pwudence who can wead."

"Rosabella!" whooped Solly. "You are the best, the cleverest, the most amazing child ever!"

"I know," said the Prodigy.

"Congratulations, Rosabella," said Prudence. "You are now the owner of the most boring pet in the world."

"Di'n't I do good?" said the Prodigy with a pout. Solly gave Prudence a nudge.

"Yes," said Prudence grudgingly. "You did. But don't let it go to your head. Come on, Solly, get a move on."

Solly hurried to the door and attempted to insert the key into the lock. His hands were so numb, he couldn't feel it.

"Hurry up," said Prudence. "What are you doing?"

"I'm trying to get it in," muttered Solly. "It doesn't seem to want to go."

"Perhaps it's the wrong key after all."

"No, I'm sure it's right. But there's something stopping it."

"Ice," said the Prodigy from behind.

"What?"

"It's fwozen. The lock on our cawavan gets fwozen sometimes. We get Fwank to come an' blow on it."

"Fwank?"

"He's the fire-eater. The Amazin' Flambo. If he's busy, we bweave on it ourselves wiv our hot bweaf."

"Excellent idea," said Solly. The Prodigy was coming up with all sorts of useful stuff these days. "Right. Here goes, then. Take the key, Prudence."

Prudence took the key. Solly knelt down on the cold, hard cobbles, puckered his lips, placed them firmly over the keyhole, and blew.

"That should do it," said Prudence after a minute or two. Solly remained where he was.

"Come on," she said after another minute. "It must be unfrozen now."

"Ooshtug," said Solly. His muffled voice was coming from far back in his throat.

"What?"

"Ooshtug!"

"What?"

"Ooshtug! Oolooshishtug!"

He rolled his eyes and gesticulated wildly, pointing to his puckered lips.

"He says his lips is stuck," said the Prodigy with a little giggle. "Fwoze to the lock. That happened to Uncle Mad once. Half his mustache comed off when we got him fwee."

"Goodness," said Prudence. "What shall we do? Just yank him away, really quickly?"

"Gno!" shouted Solly. "Gonoogare!"

"He says we're not to dare," translated the Prodigy.

"Why not? It gets it over quickly. Just one short, sharp, agonizing pain and—"

"Gno!"

"He says no," interpreted the Prodigy.

"Well, we've got to do something. He can't stay there all night. Come on, Solly. Try. Just gently pull your head back a bit."

"Gno! Gy gissle gungoch!"

"He says his lips'll come off," clarified the Prodigy. Adding, darkly, "They will, too."

"Oh, bother!" Prudence stamped her foot on the cobbles. "This is just too ridiculous. It'd never happen to Bugless. Why is real life so complicated? There must be an answer. There'll be trouble if the night watch catches us here."

"Hot water," said the Prodigy. She had found a frostbitten carrot and was feeding it to Mr. Skippy. It was the first time he had shown any sign of enthusiasm. Vigorous crunching sounds echoed around the alley. She gave a happy little shriek. "Look! Mr. Skippy's eatin'!"

"We'll be in hot water all right," agreed Prudence.

"No," said the Prodigy, "I mean *weal* hot water. If we had some, it'd melt the ice. Go on, Mr. Skippy, have some more."

"Good thinking," admitted Prudence after due consideration. "But where are we to get hot water this time of night?"

"What would happen in one of your storwies?"

"Well, that's obvious. If I wrote myself into such a stupid corner, which I wouldn't, but if I did, I'd probably have some unexpected savior come along. A kindly old chestnut seller with a handy brazier or something. But this isn't a story, and—"

"'Scuse me?" said a high voice. It came from behind the pile of rubbish. Prudence and the Prodigy both gasped and whirled around. Poor Solly couldn't, of course. He just knelt there with his lips glued to the lock, feeling more foolish than he had ever felt in his life.

A section of the rubbish heap gave a convulsive heave. Then, to their horror, a shadowy shape arose, causing a small avalanche of bottles, sodden boxes, and old potato peelings.

The shadowy shape began to move toward them. Prudence raised her basket. The Prodigy hugged Mr. Skippy defensively.

The shadowy shape came ever closer, finally revealing itself to be…

A boy. A boy wearing the most unbelievable collection of filthy rags they had ever seen. His feet were bare. His hair stuck up in wild disarray. The whites of his eyes gleamed out from layers of thick, sooty grime. If there was a Dirtiest Boy Contest, he would have won Best in Show. Despite his unpromising appearance, he was grinning. It was an uncertain grin, but it was a grin all the same. His teeth flashed white in the starlight.

"Evenin', all," said the Dirtiest Boy in the World. "I'm Freddy."

LARRIKINS!

In which Freddy proves useful,
Solly is freed, and the
Prodigy is left on guard.

The newcomer shuffled from bare foot to bare foot, scratching himself and maintaining his cheery grin while the girls stared him up and down. He had an air of hopeful anticipation, as though poised on somebody's doorstep waiting for an invitation to come in for lemonade and cake.

The Prodigy recovered first. She was used to unusual sights, being in the traveling extravaganza business.

"Hello," she said. "I's Little Wosabella. I got a wabbit under my blanket." Proudly, she swept the blanket aside.

"Yer?" said the newcomer. "Well, that's a right pretty name, an' no mistake. An' that rabbit's a beauty. Fact is, I don't fink I seen a better-lookin' rabbit. Larrikins! That's a king among rabbits, that is." He stretched out a filthy hand and gave Mr. Skippy's ear a little stroke.

Mr. Skippy just stared straight ahead. He had finished the carrot and lost interest in life again.

"He talks, but only to me," the Prodigy informed the newcomer.

"He does? Well, I never!"

"He says he likes you."

"Well, I'm right glad to 'ear it."

"The one with her mouf open's Pwudence," went on the Prodigy, pointing at Prudence, who was indeed open-jawed, still in shock. "She's witin' a book. An' the one on the gwound's Solly. Say hello to Fweddy, Solly."

"Ooh-ooh!" wailed Solly. Every syllable was agony. "Ow. Helgnee."

"His lips is stuck," the Prodigy informed Freddy. "He's sayin' 'help me.' Do you fink I's pwetty?"

"Enough!"

Prudence had finally found her voice.

"What are you doing here, boy?" she asked. "Have you been spying on us?"

"No, Miss. I was asleep, Miss."

"I see. And do you usually sleep in a pile of rubbish?"

"Oh, yes, Miss!" said Freddy. "Keeps me warm, see. The further you're in, the better it gets.

Real cozy, rubbish. A lot o' people don't know that."

"Smelly, though," said the Prodigy, wrinkling her small nose. Freddy's aroma was pungent, to say the least.

"Oh, you gets used to that," said Freddy cheerfully. "Larrikins! I'll sleep through anything— though to tell the truth, by rights I shouldn't 'ave bin sleepin'." Boss told me to keep an eye on the brush while he went to the tavern."

"Boss being . . . ?" inquired Prudence.

"Jonas Scurvy, the sweep. I'm his boy. Larrikins! I'll be in for it if he catches me talkin' to you."

Over by the keyhole, it was all getting too much for Solly. His knees were killing him where the cobbles pressed in. His frozen blood had come to a standstill, and his bones ached unbearably. But worse than anything were his lips. If his head wobbled even a little bit, the agony was indescribable.

"Ngah," he moaned. "Hoogoggy googunging, gleeg!"

"He says 'Somebody do somethin', please.'" translated the Prodigy, popping another sweet into her mouth and sucking happily. "Poor Solly," she added.

"Stuck, you say?" Freddy pattered across the freezing cobbles and bent down to have a closer look. "Cor, see what you mean. Larrikins! That's a fine pickle you got into, guv, an' no mistake."

"Gigo," groaned Solly, rolling his eyes.

"He knows," the Prodigy told them sadly.

"Still. Look on the bright side, eh? That's what I always do."

Solly couldn't see a bright side. All he could see was door. But it hurt too much to say so.

"Hot water's what we need," said Prudence. "I don't suppose you . . . ?"

That was all it took. Freddy was off and running down the alley, his unwashed bare feet barely touching the cobbles. He paused briefly at the corner and gave a jaunty little wave.

"Wait there!" he shouted. And was gone.

"Well!" said Prudence. "Wasn't that the strangest thing?"

"Now what?" asked the Prodigy.

"We wait. Nothing else to do. Pass the sweets."

Over by the lock, Solly let out a tortured moan.

Mercifully, it wasn't long before Freddy returned. He wasn't running this time. He was walking fast, though, holding something carefully in his hands. Prudence and the Prodigy ran to meet him. Solly, of course, stayed right where he was.

"Hot water?" asked Prudence, staring down at the small bowl.

"Soup," said Freddy proudly. "Cabbage. Got it from the soup kitchen behind the warehouse."

"It smells howwible," commented the Prodigy.

"What, this? Cor, lovely, this is. Larrikins! Big treat o' the day. They gives it out free in winter. One bowl each. I 'ad mine earlier. Ain't s'posed to go back for more, but the cook knows me, see?" Freddy put a dirty finger on one side of his nose and gave a little wink.

"But it's all gweasy."

"Ah. Well, it's the grease what does you good, see."

"Will soup work, do you think?" asked Prudence.

"Should do. 'Ot, ain't it? Well, it were when I started out. Coolin' off a bit now."

"We'd best get cracking then," said Prudence, taking the bowl. "Solly?"

"Groo?" Solly rolled anguished eyes.

"I'm going to pour tepid, greasy cabbage soup on your lips."

"Gogugygo! Gogugygo!"

"He says not up his nose," the Prodigy informed everyone.

"I heard," said Prudence. "Trust me, Solly. I promise I won't get it up your nose. Ready?"

"Gnng."

"Here goes, then. Out of the way, you two."

Obediently, Freddy and the Prodigy stood back.

With no more ado, Prudence tilted the bowl. Warm slop coursed down Solly's face. It ran in his eyes. It ran through his hair and dripped off his ears. Despite Prudence's promise, quite a lot of it went up his nose. For one terrible moment, he thought he'd never breathe again. He would drown in cabbage soup. What a way to go. And then . . .

He was free! His lips parted from the lock and he fell back, clutching at his oh-so-tender mouth.

The Prodigy cheered, and Freddy did an impromptu little caper on the spot.

"Ow! Ow, ow, ow!" howled Solly, rolling in an icy puddle.

"Solly!" cried the Prodigy, thrusting Mr. Skippy into Freddy's arms and running to him. "Is you all wight?"

"No. Ow. Cripes, that hurt! They're all peeled, look, see?"

"Poor, poor Solly." The Prodigy crouched down and wiped soup from his eyes with the edge of her blanket.

"They're fine," said Prudence, never known for her sympathy. "They'll hurt for a bit, but that's normal. We've wasted quite enough time on your silly lip crisis. I'm going to try the key again. Out of the way."

She pushed past him, took the key from her pocket, inserted it into the lock, and turned it. There was a scraping noise, followed by a satisfying click. She pushed on the door, and it swung inward with a squeal, revealing a pitch-black interior.

"Right," she said. "I'm going in. Coming?"

"Can I have a sweet, Rosabella?" begged Solly, humbly. "For strength? I think it might help."

"There's only two left."

"Can I have one then? I am owed."

"All wight. Not the wed one—I's savin' it."

Solly took the last green sweet and popped it in, making sure he didn't touch his skinned lips.

It helped.

With a huge effort of will, he forced life into his frozen limbs and climbed to his feet. Groaning, he bent down and rubbed his pitted knees. They felt lumpy, like old cauliflowers.

"Come *on,*" said Prudence. "If we're going in, let's go."

"What about me an' Mr. Skippy?" asked the Prodigy, collecting her pet from Freddy.

"Stay out here and guard. You can't come in, because you steal things. If anyone comes, whistle."

"I can't whistle."

"Then cough. Anything but sing."

"But it's cweepy out here!"

"It's worse inside. Pawnbrokers always keep old skeletons behind the counter. Of murdered shop-lifters."

"All wight." The Prodigy changed her mind and sat down on the curb. "Mr. Skippy says we'll guard."

"What about me?" asked Freddy. He was hovering hopefully on the fringe, desperately eager to be involved, but everyone seemed to have forgotten about him.

"It's all right," said Prudence. "You've done your bit."

"I'd like to help, an' no mistake."

"Really, we're fine. You can go now."

Still Freddy hovered. Prudence waved him away, and he backed off a few steps. His eager eyes stayed fixed on her face, though.

"That's a bit hard, isn't it?" protested Solly under his breath.

"Is it? Why?"

"Well, you can't just use people and dump them like that. Bugless might, but I wouldn't."

Solly felt very strongly on this point. He knew all about being dumped. Besides, he felt particularly well disposed toward Freddy. After all, if it hadn't been for him, his lips would still be glued to the lock. Probably minus the rest of his face, if Prudence had had her forcible way.

"But we're all right on our own," argued Prudence. "We don't need him. He's got his own problems. He sleeps in rubbish. He's got a master with a horrible-sounding name who could be back anytime. He'll only complicate things. We'll end up having to sort out his life as well as our own. He'll be a nuisance."

"Shhh. Keep your voice down. He'll hear and get upset."

"So what? We don't know him. We're already stuck with a runaway circus child and a useless rabbit. Besides, he says 'larrikins' all the time. That could get very irritating after a while."

"He wants to help. So let him," argued Solly.

"Me an' Mr. Skippy don't want Fweddy to go," said the Prodigy from the curb. She waggled Mr. Skippy's furry head from side to side. "You see? He's shakin' his head."

Prudence nibbled on her pencil. Six eyes were on her. Eight, if you included the rabbit. There was nothing to do but give in.

"All right," she said with a sigh. "He can strike the matches."

"Cor!" Freddy brightened instantly. "Can I?"

"But I don't want any nonsense involving your boss, agreed? We've got enough problems. We can't spare the time."

"Done!"

"Now, let's go."

And the three of them were swallowed into the darkness of the shop. The Prodigy was left all alone in the cold, dark alley, cuddling Mr. Skippy.

With nothing better to do, the Prodigy decided to teach him how to hop. She took him from under her blanket and placed him on the cobbles. He just sat.

"Hop, Mr. Skippy," said the Prodigy.

Mr. Skippy didn't move a muscle. He clearly needed some encouragement.

The Prodigy reached into the split bag of vegetable peelings, found another frostbitten carrot, and threw it. It landed with a clunk, then rolled off into the shadows.

That did the trick. Mr. Skippy raised his head and sniffed the air.

"Hop, Mr. Skippy," commanded the Prodigy again.

And Mr. Skippy hopped. Once. Twice. Three times. Following the smell. Into the shadows.

Straight into a boot.

Once inside the shop, Solly, Prudence, and Freddy didn't waste time. Freddy scrabbled beneath the counter, located a candle, and had it alight in seconds. Solly gave Prudence a leg up onto the counter, then stood picking cabbage out of his hair and patting his sore lips.

Prudence ran her practiced eyes over the shelf

of old ledgers. Freddy held the candle high and steady so that she could see what she was doing.

In a matter of seconds, she found the one she wanted. She pulled it out and knelt on the counter, flipping over yellowing pages and running her finger down long columns of spidery writing. Finally, she gave a little grunt of satisfaction.

"Here we are. Listen. 'One silver spoon, excellent condition. Engraved with the initials *V.I.P.* Pawned by one Arnold Scubbins on November 9. Pawn ticket number 307. Price paid: six shillings. Sold November 10 to Mrs. Irma Spindletrap of Thrift House. Price received: thirty shillings.' See? What did I say? He sold it the very next day, for five times the amount he paid for it."

"V.I.P.," breathed Solly. "Wow! That's me! What do you think the letters stand for?"

"Could be anything," said Prudence. "Valerian Isambard Proud? Victor Inigo Plockett? Vincent Ivor Poodleflower?"

Solly nodded eagerly. Any of those would do nicely. Except, perhaps, the last one.

"Thrift 'Ouse," said Freddy. "That's the town orphanage. They say it's an orful place."

"Really?" said Prudence. "Hear that, Solly? Next stop, Orful Orphanage."

Solly wasn't listening. He was still thinking about his spoon. Not only was it engraved; it was worth a small fortune. Thirty shillings! He couldn't get his head around such a huge sum. Was his real family royalty, or what?

Prudence slammed the ledger shut, stuffed it back on the shelf, and jumped down. Freddy blew out the candle and carefully put it back where he had found it, then the three of them hurried from the shop.

"We'd better lock the door," Prudence was saying. "Old Pinchpenny won't even know we've—"

She stopped. Solly and Freddy piled up behind her.

"What the—" began Solly.

"Larrikins!" whispered Freddy from the rear.

Standing in the alley was the group of disreputable youths they had seen earlier that day hanging around the lamppost!

There were three of them. One looked like a toad, with blubbery lips and a thick neck. He held a stout cudgel in his hand. One was small and weaselly, with missing teeth. He was holding

Mr. Skippy by his ears. The third was tall and thin, like a scarecrow, with long straggly hair caught back in a ponytail. He wore a ragged corduroy frock coat and a battered stovepipe hat. He was smiling. It wasn't nice.

Worst of all—his hand was clamped over the Prodigy's rosebud mouth! Her startled eyes rose over his dirty fingers.

"Evening, kiddies," drawled the Scarecrow, raising a thin eyebrow.

"Now, look here . . ." began Solly.

"If you think you can—" began Prudence. But the Scarecrow cut them off.

"You!" He nodded curtly at Freddy. "You cut an' run. I don't want no trouble with Jonas Scurvy."

Freddy didn't need telling twice. In the blink of an eye, he was gone.

"Right." The Scarecrow threw the Prodigy's blanket up over her head, picked her up, and tucked her under his arm. "Time for a walk."

YOU'RE *MY* CHILDREN NOW

❧ ❧

In which the Intelligent Reader
will be concerned to learn that
our heroes are kidnapped, and
the Prodigy is silenced, for once.

I don't believe this is happening," muttered Solly as they stumbled along. He was colder than ever. His feet hurt. His lips throbbed. His hair smelled of cabbage. His engraved, thirty-shilling silver spoon was receding ever further into the distance. Things couldn't get any worse. Or could they?

They were being hustled along yet another dark alleyway. It looked just like the last one, and the one before that, and the one before *that*.

The order they proceeded in was as follows: the Scarecrow first, with the bundled-up Prodigy clamped beneath one arm. Her little blue boots stuck out, wiggling feebly. She couldn't even do one of her famous screams, because her mouth was stuffed full of blanket.

Next came the Weasel, with the dangling Mr. Skippy. Any animal with half a brain would have thrashed and wriggled, desperate to get away. Mr. Skippy just hung from his ears like a limp fur sack.

After the weasel came Solly, followed by Prudence. The Toad brought up the rear, thumping his stick into the palm of his hand with a sinister *thwack*.

"Where d'you think they're taking us?" hissed Solly from the corner of his mouth as they turned yet another corner.

"Probably some sort of thieves' den," muttered Prudence. "They'll train us to become pickpockets, like in *Gulliver Twitt*. There'll be this old man called Fargin or Feegle or something like that. He'll live in an attic with dozens of chirpy children who sing songs to keep their spirits up."

"Cripes. Do you really think so?"

"Either that or straightforward child slavery in a factory."

"What?"

"Or maybe down a mine."

"Does that involve crawling along on your knees?" Solly didn't think his knees could take much more.

"There you go, moaning again," said Prudence, adding, "Bugless wouldn't."

"Oi! Big nose! Shut yer trap!" ordered the Toad.

Prudence gave him a poisonous look and opened her mouth to object. Solly nudged her in the ribs, nodding at the cudgel. Reluctantly, she subsided.

Boots slipping and sliding on the icy cobbles, they trudged on. Then, "'Ere we all are," said the Scarecrow. "'Ome again, 'ome again, jiggetty jig."

He had stopped before a tall, thin building halfway down the alley. It looked very similar to all the other buildings they had passed. Dark. Silent. Ominous.

The Scarecrow hoisted the bundled Prodigy higher under his arm, then rapped out a complicated series of taps on the peeling front door. After a short pause, it creaked open a fraction. A low voice muttered something. The Scarecrow muttered something back. There came the sound of receding footsteps.

"In we all go, then," said the Scarecrow.

Hearts in their mouths, Solly and Prudence stepped over the threshold. Inside, a steep flight of narrow stairs ascended into darkness.

"Me an' you'll go on up with the little 'un," said the Scarecrow to the Weasel. "The small ones fetch a better price." He turned to the Toad. "Tonks, you guard the other two. Send 'em up when I gives the word."

With that, he turned and began to climb the stairs two at a time, looking for all the world like a spider scuttling up its web with a trussed fly. The Weasel followed. The last thing Solly saw was Mr. Skippy's white tail disappearing into the shadows.

The Toad gave a leer, leaned against the door, took a half-eaten, mold-covered piece of fruitcake from his pocket, and began to eat with relish.

"Go on, then," whispered Solly to Prudence.

"What?"

"Tell me what Bugless would do. That's what you usually do in these situations."

"Only because you ask."

"All right. So I'm asking."

"Well, of course, he'd do something heroic. Like grab the cudgel and fight his way out."

"I see," said Solly, eyeing the Toad's cudgel. "Yes. I see. Interesting. Foolish, but interesting."

"Don't worry," said Prudence. "This is a case where life shouldn't mirror fiction. You're not up to it."

Solly didn't know whether to be grateful or huffy. Was she referring to his injuries or his lack of heroic qualities? He suspected the latter.

"Oi!" said the Toad, downing the last of his

moldy cake. He pointed with the cudgel. "Shut it, I said."

Solly and Prudence shut it. All three waited in silence at the foot of the stairs. Eventually, the Scarecrow's voice came drifting down.

"All right, Tonks. She'll take 'em as a job lot. Send 'em up."

"Git crackin'," ordered the Toad with a leer.

She? Thought Solly as he dragged himself up the creaking steps, with Prudence in his wake. Who's she?

He didn't have long to wait to find out.

The flight of steps ended in a long passageway lined with doors. The one at the end was open. To Solly's surprise, a mellow, welcoming light streamed out. The Scarecrow leaned against the doorjamb, looking pleased with himself and tossing a bag full of clinking coins from one hand to the other.

"In you go, my little friends," he said, sweeping off his hat and giving a low, mocking bow. "Nanny awaits."

Solly and Prudence eyed each other. There was nothing else to do. They stepped in.

Inside, it was—oh, bliss!—warm. Hot, in fact. So hot and stuffy, it almost hurt.

Solly stared around. It certainly wasn't what he had been expecting.

A huge, crackling fire blazed at one end of the room. Before it was a rocking chair, in which there sat a tiny woman. Her round, pink face was smiling. She looked like a storybook version of the perfect granny—but pintsize. She had the gray corkscrew curls, the frilly cap, the shawl, the spectacles, everything down to a bag of knitting at her feet. On her lap sat the Prodigy, looking confused and rather sleepy. Her arms were wrapped around Mr. Skippy.

"Come in!" cried the little woman, beaming and beckoning with a minute hand. "Nanny's got a lovely fire going. Come and warm yourselves, my angels—you look froze half to death."

Warily, Solly and Prudence moved farther into the room. The heat enveloped them like a blanket. Already their hands and feet were beginning to tingle.

There was a knock on the door behind them, and the Weasel sidled in, cap in hand.

"I put the milk on, like you said, Nanny," he said gruffly, eyes on the floor. "Can I go now?"

"Thank you, Spinks, dear. That was very kind of you. All right, off you go. We've done our business. Tell Tonks to make sure he locks and bolts the front door properly. And tell Spider to keep the supply coming. Nanny's got three more little beds all ready and waiting."

The Weasel scuttled out the door. Two sets of footsteps clattered down the stairs.

"My Boys," said Nanny, beaming. "So good to me. Live downstairs. Stop naughty people coming in. And going out, of course. You can't be too careful around these parts."

Solly continued staring around the room. It was laid out like a nursery. Six neatly made-up beds were lined up against a wall. They had pink-and-white checked coverlets. The windows were hung with matching curtains. There was a rug on the floor and pictures on the wall—mostly of small children playing with puppies and kittens.

There were toys, too. A wooden rocking horse with a flowing mane. A doll's house. A pile of boxed jigsaw puzzles. A fort with tin soldiers. A farmyard, complete with tiny animals. A Noah's ark. A set of building blocks . . .

. . . and dolls. Rows of beautifully dressed dolls, carefully arranged on shelves, their blank eyes catching the firelight.

"My babies. Lovely, aren't they?" said Nanny, seeing him look. "Your sisters can hold them tomorrow, if they're careful. You can play with the fort, if you're a good boy. But tonight, you need supper and a good night's sleep. Little children need their rest."

"Look," said Prudence. "Would you mind telling us what's going on?"

"My, my!" Nanny was shocked. "Aren't we forgetting something?"

"No, I think that about covers it."

"I was referring to 'please.'"

"All right. Please, then."

"That's better. We don't have rudeness in my nursery. But if you're good, Nanny's got everything happy little children need. Right, Rosabella, my angel, down you go. Time for a milky drink and some supper. It's all ready. You can sit in my chair. Nanny loves little children. Oh yes."

And with that, she bustled from the room, shutting the door behind her. There came the sound of a key turning, followed by receding footsteps.

"I don't see any singing pickpockets," Solly said to Prudence. "You were wrong there, Prudence."

Prudence said nothing. She was wandering around, picking up toys and putting them down again. The Prodigy was asleep and snoring in the rocking chair, bonnet askew.

"At least it's warm," went on Solly, holding out his hands to the flames. "And I could certainly do with some supper."

"Hmm." Prudence walked to a window and twitched back the curtain. "Bars."

"What?"

"The window's barred. See?" She pulled on her nose. "I don't like this. The sooner we get out of here the better."

"But can't we eat first?" pleaded Solly.

"No. Show a bit of backbone. We're on a quest for your spoon. We can't afford to be sidetracked."

"Well, I know, but—"

"Spoon or supper? Which is it to be?"

"Well, I know which Bugless'd choose, of course.

He can probably run for weeks on a tadpole sandwich—"

"I'm asking you."

"All right, all right. Spoon, then."

It was the right choice, of course. But he said it rather grumpily.

There came the sound of the key rattling in the lock. The door opened again, to admit Nanny with a groaning tray.

"Nursery food," she announced, beaming. "Nanny knows what little children like."

Solly's eyes fixed on the tray. Food! Real food! Food that wasn't pottage! And not a turnip to be seen! Instead, crumbly pudding. A jug of something hot and yellow. And—was it?—yes! Bread and butter! Slice after slice, with the crusts cut off! With a dish of—honey! It had to be honey! And what in the world was that heavenly-looking wobbly red stuff?

Prudence gave him a nudge and muttered, "Stop drooling and be strong."

"Come on, then, dearies," said Nanny, all smiles. "Draw up a couple of stools to the fire. I want to see clean plates, mind."

"We're not staying," said Prudence.

"Oh?" Nanny's eyebrows shot up. "And why is that?"

"We have to be somewhere. Don't we, Solly?"

"Mmm?" Solly dragged him unwilling eyes from the wobbly red stuff. "Oh—yes. We have to go."

"What, out into the cold night? On empty tummies? Without mittens?"

"We'll be fine," insisted Prudence. "Solly, wake up Rosabella. We're going."

"Stay where you are, young man!" Suddenly Nanny didn't sound quite so cozy. "Nobody's going anywhere tonight. You're staying here with Nanny."

"Look," said Prudence, "if you think you can keep us here against our wi—"

"Are you arguing with me, Miss?" Nanny put down the tray and waggled a reproving finger. "I *do* hope not."

Solly felt he should back Prudence up.

"Prudence is right," he said. "We really must be off."

"Oh dear," sighed Nanny. "Now we've got a naughty little *boy* arguing with Nanny. This won't do. It won't do at all. I can see we need to be taught some manners. But first things first. Eat your supper up. Then Tonks will bring up the tub and we'll see about your baths."

"Bath?" Solly felt a sudden twinge of uncertainty. He had never had a bath in his life, and he certainly wasn't about to start now, in front of a complete stranger, with girls about.

"Oh, yes. We can't go to bed all dirty, can we?"

"I don't want a bath, thanks very much."

"Ah, but it's not what *you* want, is it? It's what Nanny wants. You see"—she beamed up at him, the firelight reflecting in her glasses—"you see, you're *my* children now."

PERFECT PARENTS
INTERLUDE FOUR

In which Lady Elvira makes out
invitations to her dinner guests.

Lady Elvira sat at her writing desk. It overlooked the ornamental lake, which was beginning to freeze over. The sky was gray and heavy. It looked like snow was on the way.

Sighing, her Ladyship dipped her pen into a silver inkwell and signed the final invitation. She didn't feel like visitors, but then, she never felt like anything much.

"All done, darling?" inquired her husband, appearing in the doorway. He wore his top hat and heavy overcoat. In one hand, he held a silver-topped cane.

"Yes, dearest. I've invited everyone you suggested."

"Excellent," said his Lordship, gathering up the envelopes. "I'll mail them on the way to the club. An

evening of convivial company should put the roses back in your cheeks, eh?"

"Maybe. Of course, not a second will go by when I am not thinking of our dear boy. But I will do my best to be merry."

"I know you will. I'll send in cook to discuss the menu, shall I?"

"Very well. Goodbye, Charles."

"Goodbye, darling. Chin up, eh?"

Lady Elvira waited until the door closed behind him. Then she buried her head in her hands and once again gave in to sorrow.

HELP!
WE ARE PRISONERS

❧

In which time is spent in
Nanny's nursery and an ingenious
escape plan is hatched,
which involves everybody
making a sacrifice.

I f I have to spend one more second in this place," announced Prudence, "I shall go barking mad."

"That makes two of us," agreed Solly.

"Thwee," growled the Prodigy.

"We've got to get out of here!" stormed Prudence. "I can't eat more jam—I just can't! What's she trying to do? Fatten us up or something?"

"Like a howwid ole witch," added the Prodigy darkly.

The three of them were having a morning council of war. The curtains had been pulled back, revealing the barred window. Far below lay the deserted alleyway. Ahead, jumbled rooftops and tall chimneys were silhouetted against a gray wintry sky.

It was the first time they had had the opportunity to have a proper talk. The night before, private conversation had proved impossible. Nanny ran her nursery with an iron fist when it came to talking after lights out. Not that they'd felt like talking anyway, after the rich, sugary meal, which had been wonderful at first, but not so good later. And then—

Oh, horror! The bath.

The bath. Nanny had made them all have one before bed. First the Prodigy, who had snored throughout. Then Prudence. Then Solly. All right, so she had pulled a screen over and all three of them had politely looked the other way when the others had their turns, but it had still been utterly humiliating, trying to keep one's dignity with the aid of a small towel while a strange midget poured jugs of water from on high and insisted on inspecting ears. After that, there was nothing to do but put on the stiff white cotton nightshirt pro-vided, climb into the (admittedly) comfy bed, and welcome the oblivion of deep, exhausted sleep.

Mind you, waking up had been no picnic. Living with Nanny was, quite frankly, awful.

Right now, Solly was slumped face-down on his bed, feeling sick. For the first time ever, he knew what it felt like to eat too much. All his life he had dreamed of this, but he had never realized how quickly the novelty would wear off.

They had been woken shortly after dawn with a groaning tray. All morning, meals kept coming. Breakfast, brunch, lunch. Muffins and toast and jam and rice pudding and endless mugs of milky drinks. Everything had to be eaten or you got scolded and threatened with the Boys, who lived downstairs and were clearly employed in a strong-arm capacity. Mutiny was out of the question.

To make Solly feel even sicker, he was wearing a sailor suit! When he had opened his eyes first thing in the morning, there it was, all neatly pressed and waiting for him. It was white, trimmed with blue, and clearly designed to fit a seven-year-old. It was so tight across the chest, he could hardly breathe. The trousers kept riding up, show-ing acres of bare leg. And the hat! He had caught sight of himself in the nursery mirror and nearly died. Luckily, the girls were kind enough not to laugh, although he could see it was an effort.

Mind you, they had their own problems.

Prudence stood by the window, drumming her knuckles on the sill. She was wearing a white dress with a lace collar, which she claimed itched. The dress was ridiculously small and looked ludicrous teamed with her huge boots. Her wrists stuck out miles beyond the cuffs. She was in a terrible, terrible mood.

The Prodigy sat scowling in the rocking chair, hugging Mr. Skippy, recovering from a major temper tantrum. At her feet lay a china doll. Its dress was torn, and one of its arms was missing. The Prodigy was furious because Nanny had dressed her all in green, which she claimed didn't suit her. She had tried screaming and got a smack. She had then attempted to attack Nanny with her little blue parasol. Nanny had promptly confiscated it, along with the Prodigy's blanket and all her blue clothes, claiming that they were fit only for the rag-and-bone man.

Then—oh, deary me! Then Nanny had turned her attention to Prudence's basket. She found the crow-scarer, the matches, the candle stub, the sixpence—and, worst of all, the precious composition book containing *Little Sir Thummagain*. What a fuss that had caused, particularly when Nanny declared that writing silly stories wasn't a suitable occupation for girls. She had had to call in the Boys for reinforcements. Despite Prudence's furious objections, the basket had been forcibly removed, along with her pencil. Nanny had then bundled up the rest of their old clothes, leaving them only their boots and the horrible new outfits she had provided.

Mind you, she hadn't gotten Solly's cloth. Wisely, seeing what was happening to the girls and their things, he had untied it from his neck and slipped it under his mattress. He wasn't about to give that up in a hurry.

"Well," said Solly, rolling over and holding his stomach, "she's locked the door, the window only opens a tiny way, and there are bars. We're way above street level, and if we try shouting for help, she'll hear us. Ow—my stomach really hurts."

"Don't want to be wescued wearin' gween anyway," sulked the Prodigy.

"I hate her!" raged Prudence. "Just look at this dress! I'm a joke!"

"At least it's not gween."

"Well, we've got to do something. Next time she arrives with another trayload, let's just overpower her, ram her head in the treacle pudding, and make a run for it. That's what Bugless would do."

"Really?" said Solly. "Well, I must say I'm disappointed in him. It wouldn't work. He'd run straight into the Boys. Besides, the street door's sure to be locked. It's a lousy idea."

Prudence considered.

"All right, then. He'd write a note and throw it down. Obviously, it would get picked up by a passerby, who would alert the authorities."

"It'd blow away in the wind," objected Solly. It felt quite good to be one up on Bugless, for once. "You'd think he'd have thought of that."

"All right, then, he'd tie it to something heavy and lower it down. Using a rope cunningly made from torn-up sheets. And a passerby would trip over it."

"Hmm." Solly considered. "Not a bad idea. But how do we write a note? We haven't got a pencil. Or paper."

"Don't remind me," said Prudence bitterly, through gritted teeth. "I've looked everywhere. No crayons, no chalk, nothing. Just dolls and stuff."

"Of course," Solly went on, "there are other ways of writing a note. Didn't I see a sewing basket among the toys? With needles and thread and stuff?"

"I think so. Why?"

"Well, you could sew a message. On a bit of

cloth. Something like 'Help. Look up. We are pris-
oners. Get police.'"

Prudence's face was a mask of horror.

"Me?" she said. "You want me to sew?"

"Well, yes."

"But I hate sewing."

"I know."

"It took me three years to do a *P*."

"I know, I know. But it doesn't have to be perfect. Just so you can read it. Do big stitches."

Prudence sighed deeply.

"All right," she agreed. "But I hope you know it
goes right against my principles."

"We all have to make sacrifices for the cause,"
explained Solly.

"In that case, give me your napkin."

"What?"

"I'll use your napkin for the message. It's ideal."

"I'm not so sure about that. . . ."

"I thought you said we all have to make sacrifices. Anyway, you rely too much on that stupid old
cloth. Bugless wouldn't. Come on. Give."

Stung, Solly reached under the mattress, pulled

out his cloth and handed it over. His hand hardly shook.

"What we goin' to use for the heavy fing to wap the note awound?" broke in the Prodigy. She was stroking Mr. Skippy's ears. He was slumped stolidly on her lap, doing nothing as usual. "A bwick or somefin?"

"No," said Solly. "It's got to be something soft and bendy. Something that will squeeze through the bars, but with a bit of weight. It needs to be something unusual, that'll attract attention. Something like . . ."

He paused.

"What?" asked the Prodigy.

"Something like . . ."

"What?"

"Like Mr. Skippy."

"Perfect," agreed Prudence. "Why didn't I think of that?"

"Nooooo!" wailed the Prodigy, hugging her loved one fiercely. "I won't let you! He says he doesn't want to be lowered on a wope."

"Nonsense," said Prudence. "It's time the stupid thing earned its keep."

"Nooooooooo!"

"He'll be fine," cut in Solly. Prudence was good at reading and writing, but she really didn't know how to handle people. "It'll be fun for him. He'll be like a jolly little circus rabbit. If Prudence can sew and I can give up my crumb-catching cloth, you can do without Mr. Skippy for a little while, can't you? He's sure to be spotted right away. Nobody would walk straight past a rabbit wearing a napkin. We'll be rescued in no time."

"*Noooooooo . . .*"

"And then we can go and buy sweets."

" *. . . oooooo.* Pwomise?"

"Promise."

"All wight," agreed the Prodigy. But she still sounded miserable.

Some time later, the key turned and Nanny popped her head around the door.

"There's good children," she said. "Playing nicely, I see."

All three were sitting innocently on the floor. The Prodigy was dressing Mr. Skippy in a doll's hat. Prudence was looking at a picture book. Solly was briskly polishing the miniature cannon from the toy fort.

"I'll get one of the Boys to bring up a bit more coal for that fire in a bit. It'll be out soon. It's starting to snow. We're in for a cold night. I'm just popping out for fresh scones for your tea. Good children get honey and cream."

"Thank you," said Solly. "That would be lovely."

"There's nice manners," said Nanny, beaming. "Now we're learning. Put your hat on, dear. You look sweet in it."

Solly obediently put his sailor hat on and tried to look sweet.

Her head retreated and once again the door was locked.

"Right," said Solly, hurling the hat to the floor. "Let's do it."

All three jumped into action. Prudence reached under a cushion and pulled out Solly's cloth, on which the message had been stitched in large, red, rather uneven letters. The Prodigy pulled back the cover on her bed, revealing a length of torn strips of sheet, firmly knotted together. Solly scooped up Mr. Skippy and Prudence tied the napkin around his middle. They then bundled his inert body into a makeshift sling made of a torn-up pillowcase, which they attached to the sheet-rope.

Through it all, Mr. Skippy remained emotionless, despite getting soaked by the Prodigy's copious tears.

Solly went to the window, winding the sheet-rope around his elbow. Outside, it was getting dark and beginning to snow.

"Right," he said. "Pass him over."

"Be careful," sobbed the Prodigy. "He says he don't like heights."

It was a bit of a squeeze, getting Mr. Skippy's furry body through the gap and past the bars. Luckily, he had the kind of non-personality that went with the flow. He went all limp and allowed himself to be stuffed through the opening. His eyes might have bulged a bit more than usual as he slid past the windowsill and slowly sank from view, but that was all.

The Prodigy gave a wail as the deed was done, and Mr. Skippy dropped out of sight. Slowly, little by little, Solly let the sheet-rope pass through his hands.

"Has he weached the gwound yet?" quavered the Prodigy, standing on tiptoe.

"I don't know," admitted Solly. "I can't see from here, he's too close to the wall. But we're out of sheet anyway. He can't have far to fall. And the snow'll make a soft landing. Shall I let go?"

He held the last bit of makeshift rope in his hand.

"Yes," said Prudence firmly.

"No!" wailed the Prodigy. "Bwing him back up! I's changed my mind!"

"Do it, Solly," said Prudence.

"No! I'll scweam!"

"I'm letting go," said Solly. Well, someone had to make the decision.

The last bit of sheet slipped out of his hand and slithered through the window.

"Excellent work," said Prudence. "Well done, everybody."

The Prodigy said nothing. Her blue eyes blazed with accusation. Her lower lip was trembling.

"Don't scream, Rosabella," said Solly. He exchanged an anxious glance with Prudence. "Let's all go and sit down, and Prudence will tell you a story while we're waiting to be rescued. I'll bet somebody will be along any minute. They'll see Mr. Skippy and think, ooh, what's that nice little rabbit doing all by himself in the snow. . . ."

The Prodigy took a huge breath. Her rosebud mouth opened.

"He'll be fine!" insisted Solly. "Rabbits like snow! They do, don't they, Prudence?"

"Immensely," agreed Prudence. "Nothing they like better. Haven't you heard of the Famous Snow Rabbit?" The Prodigy was turning purple. "It's a very good story."

"It is! It is!" gibbered Solly. "I thought everyone knew about the Famous Snow Rabbit. It's all about this, er, rabbit that goes out in the snow and, um, has a lovely, happy day. You've heard it, surely?"

To their great relief, the Prodigy let her breath go in a huge expulsion.

"No."

"Tell her, Prudence," urged Solly.

"Well," improvised Prudence, "there was this rabbit called—I don't know—Eustace, or something—and he loved the snow. Whenever he went out in the snow, he would wear a special hat and mittens knitted for him by his aunt Maureen."

"Were they wed ones?"

"No, green."

"I don't like gween. An' Eustace is a howwid name for a wabbit."

"Who's telling this story? Anyway—"

A sound came from behind. Guiltily, the children whirled around. Standing in the doorway, puffing heavily, was Nanny. Her glasses flashed. There was snow on her shoulders. Looming behind her were Spider, Spinks, and Tonks.

"Tut, tut," said Nanny sadly, shaking her head. "Look what landed in *my* basket!"

Slowly, she held up the basket. In it was . . .

Mr. Skippy.

He stared blankly ahead, apathetic as ever. He was obviously none the worse for his lowering experience.

The Prodigy gave a little cry and ran to her beloved. Nanny held him up higher, so she couldn't reach.

"Oh, no, you don't, Missy. We're determined to be naughty, aren't we?" She reached into the basket and withdrew Solly's napkin with the wobbly red message. She inspected it at arm's length. "Up to tricks behind Nanny's back. Not a bit grateful to

Nanny for all her kindness. I'm afraid we're going to have to be punished."

And, to Solly's horror, she marched across the room and dropped his cloth into the coals of the dying fire.

"There," she said. "That's what Nanny does with silly messages."

Solly gave a strangled croak and started forward, but Tonks and his cudgel got in the way.

"As for the rabbit . . ." She held out her basket to Spider. "It was against my better judgment to let her keep the dirty thing in the first place. Rabbits don't belong in nurseries. Chuck it out in the snow and let it freeze."

The Prodigy gave a terrible scream and launched herself at Spider. Spinks stuck his foot out and she went sprawling. Spider laughed, took the basket, turned on his heel, and left.

The Prodigy lay flat out on the floor where she had fallen, biting the rug and screeching.

Solly had had enough. More than enough.

"We want to leave," he said. "Stand aside and let us out." Nanny looked at him sharply. "Please."

He looked at Prudence and gave a helpless shrug. His manners would be the death of him.

"Give me my basket, you old goat!" hissed Prudence in a manner guaranteed not to get results.

"WAAAAAAAAH!" screamed the Prodigy, crawling about the floor. "WANT MR. SKIPPY! WAAAAAH!"

Nanny marched to the window and slammed it shut. She produced a padlock from her pocket, slipped it through the latch, and locked it.

"There," she said, returning the key to her pocket. "No more fresh air for you. And no tea. No candles. And no fire either. Tonks, collect the candles and put the fire out. We'll see how they like a night in the dark."

PERFECT PARENTS
INTERLUDE FIVE

In which the Intelligent Reader

pays another brief visit

to the Perfect Parents,

who continue to mourn.

"How the wind moans tonight," said Lady Elvira with a sigh. She was seated at her dressing table, removing her diamond earrings.

"Indeed," agreed Lord Charles, opening a drawer full of color-coordinated nightcaps. "We are in for a blizzard, I fear."

"It's nights like this I think about our boy," went on her Ladyship. "Oh, how I hope he's tucked up in a warm bed. Is he, Charles? Is he? Is he safe? Is he with people who are kind to him? Is he happy?"

"Let us hope so, dearest."

"If I only knew he was happy, I could bear it. Say he's happy, Charles. Say it!"

"Of course he is. Safe, happy, and warm. Wherever he is. . . ."

SHUFFLE YER SHOULDERS ~ NOTHING TO IT

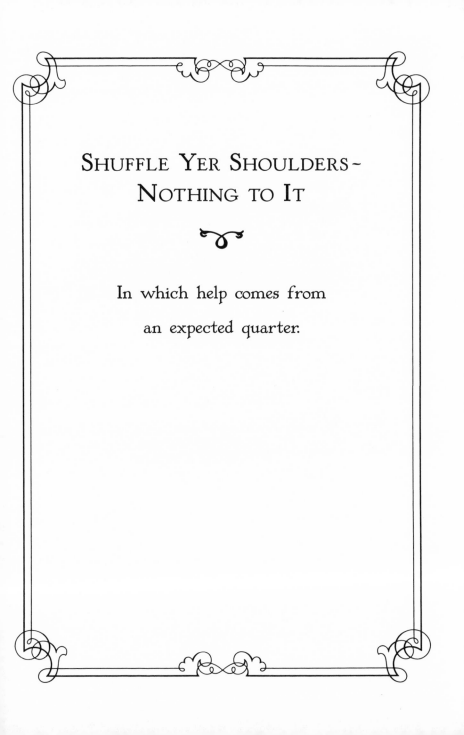

In which help comes from

an expected quarter.

No candles. No fire. No napkin. No escape. Could anything be worse? wondered Solly.

The three of them huddled together in the freezing nursery. They had removed all the blankets from the beds and piled them on the sofa in a sort of nest. The Prodigy had refused to go to bed without Mr. Skippy. She was currently fast asleep, worn out with temper and misery.

The nursery was pitch-black. Behind the curtains, frost was forming on both sides of the window. Beyond the bars, snow fell thickly.

"Thinking about your cloth?" asked Prudence, into the dark.

"No," said Solly.

"Yes, you are."

"All right, then, I am. But I'm all right. I can cope."

Could he, though? His dear old crumb-catching cloth, gone forever, consumed by fire. It felt like a bit of him was missing. Alone and nap-kinless in a cruel world.

A little silence fell. They both sighed.

"Thinking about *Little Sir Thummagain?*" asked Solly after a bit.

"Yes, if you must know."

Another pause.

"I'm sorry about all this, Prudence," said Solly. "If it wasn't for me, you'd be at the publishers getting paid right now."

"Well, not right now. Right now, it's after midnight."

"You know what I mean. All that work."

"That's all right," said Prudence. "It's not your fault. I'll write it again—that's all."

"Wow. Really? Will you remember it?"

"Oh yes. It's all in my head. But I'm thinking of making a few changes anyway. Writers need experience. All this is research. It's giving me ideas."

"It is?"

"Yes. It'll be even better next time. Cripes, it's cold in here."

She gave a shiver and moved closer to Solly. For all her brave words, she was upset about the book. He put an arm around her thin shoulders and gave her a comforting pat. He knew how she felt.

"At least Nanny's shown herself in her true colors," said Prudence. "You wait till we get out of here. I'll have her up for kidnapping, theft, force-feeding and . . . and . . . dressing people up against their will."

"In gween," mumbled the Prodigy, still sulking, even in sleep.

"What I still don't get is, why?" said Solly. "What's in it for her?"

"Well," said Prudence, "if this was a story, it'd probably turn out that she was . . ."

"Shhhh," said Solly. His heart pounded. "What's that?"

"What?"

"That noise. Listen!"

He was right. There was a scrabbling sound coming from the chimney.

"What's happenin'?" inquired the Prodigy drowsily.

"Shhhh!" hissed Solly and Prudence. All three sat bolt upright. It was too dark to make anything out, but from the sound of it, somebody—or something—was on its way down. Lumps of soot pattered down into the cold fireplace.

"Is it Father Christmas?" whispered the Prodigy. Her chilly little hand slipped into Solly's.

"Is it a burglar?" whispered Prudence.

"Probably a bird or something," said Solly, not believing a word of it.

It was none of them. As they sat clutching at each other, a match flared, a candle glowed, and a familiar voice said, "Larrikins! 'Ere you all are, right enough!"

"Freddy!" gasped Solly.

It was. He stood, grinning his ear-to-ear grin. It lit the room more than the candlelight. And that wasn't the only surprise of the night. For there, staring stolidly out from the top of his dirty shirt, inscrutable as always, was—

"Mr. Skippy!" squealed the Prodigy, bouncing to her feet.

"Yep," agreed Freddy, pulling him out and placing him carefully in the Prodigy's arms. "Out in the snow all on 'is ownio, poor little blighter. Just sittin'."

"No change there, then," said Prudence. But she sounded quite pleased.

"You wescued him!" cooed the Prodigy, showering her loved one with kisses. "Oh, clever Fweddy!"

"I got the rest of yer stuff, too," said Freddy. "Yer clothes an' that. Just dumped out in the alley, they was, along with all the rubbish. I've hidden 'em in an old warehouse down the street. Took me ages to gather 'em up an' stash 'em."

"My basket wasn't there, by any chance, was it?" asked Prudence.

"No. Sorry. But I found yer pencil. 'Ere."

He held it out. For the first time ever, Prudence smiled. It was a proper one, too. It made her look totally different. You quite forgot the nose.

"That's all right, then," she said, taking it and sticking it behind her ear. "Phew, that's better. I can think again. Well done, Freddy. You've been very helpful."

"Oh, go on!" said Freddy, blushing underneath his filth. "It weren't nothin'. I'd 'ave gotten 'ere earlier, but I 'ad to wait for the chimney to cool. Second most important rule, that."

"What's the first?" asked Solly.

"Never run away from yer governor. I've already broke that. Well, I had to, right? Couldn't let the Child Farmer get yer."

"Child Farmer?" said Prudence. "You mean—Nanny?"

"Yep. Everyone knows 'er round 'ere. Sends her boys out to pick up runaways off the street. Cleans 'em up, feeds 'em up, teaches 'em their p's an' q's an' farms 'em out."

"Who to?" asked Solly.

"Anyone who can pay. Rich folks who ain't got little uns of their own. Factory owners. Into service. She don't care, 'long as she makes a profit."

"I knew it!" said Prudence. "I just knew it was something like that. There was this story I read called *The Kidnapping of Clarence Maconker,* and—"

"Prudence," interrupted Solly. "I'm sure it's good, but perhaps now isn't the time."

"He's right," agreed Freddy. "I gotta get you outta here. Time to make the climb. I'd best go first, so as to give you a hand at the top. Lucky it's an easy one, straight up, no bends. See, you press yer knees an' elbows against the sides of the flue. Then, when yer shoulders are fixed, you shuffle yer legs up. When they're fixed, shuffle yer shoulders. Nothin' to it."

Solly and the girls looked at each other, then at the square, black, gaping hole of doom that was the fireplace.

"What's up?" asked Freddy.

"The chimney," said Solly heavily. "That's what's up. I don't think, um, I don't think the girls are too keen."

"I am," said the Prodigy. "I's good at climbin'."

"Yes, well, of course. I was thinking more of Prudence."

"No you weren't," said Prudence. "You're thinking more of *you*."

Solly went red. It was true. He wasn't good at heights. Or confined spaces. Especially in the dark, wearing a sailor suit that was too small for him. Prudence opened her mouth again. He knew what was coming.

"Don't say it, all right?" he said tightly. "I don't want to hear about Bugless right now. I suppose he'd be brilliant at climbing chimneys. Even in his pantaloons."

"He would," agreed Prudence. "He'd be up there in two shakes of a lamb's tail."

"Who's Bugless?" asked Freddy.

"Someone I'm beginning to dislike intensely," said Solly.

"Is you fwitened, Solly?" asked the Prodigy. She slipped a hand in his. "Don't wowwy. I'll help you."

This is ridiculous, thought Solly. Help from a six-year-old girl? What kind of poor sap am I, too scared to climb one little chimney? I can do it. I know I can.

But what if I can't?

"It's all right," he said, in a false, bright voice he didn't recognize. "Nothing to it, I'm sure. Let's do it." The minute he said it, he felt sick.

Freddy took Mr. Skippy from the Prodigy's arms and stuffed him back down his shirt.

"I'll take 'im," he said. "You'll need both arms. Wait till I'm up, mind, or you'll get soot in yer eyes. Larrikins! That 'urts. See you at the top."

So saying, he blew out the candle, stepped into the dark grate, gave a wink and a cheery thumbs-up, then vanished up the chimney. The last they saw was his dirty, dangling feet—then they, too, were gone.

Down below, the three of them waited. There came scuffling sounds from up the chimney. More soot fell into the fire basket. Then . . .

"All right!" came Freddy's distant voice. It echoed oddly. "Up you come, one at a time."

"Me first," said the Prodigy. And without ado, she stretched up her arms and vanished in a wiggle of green knicker-legs.

"That's it, Miss Rosabella!" Freddy's muffled voice came floating down. "Stick your elbows in. Now shuffle yer legs. That's it. Push with yer feet. Right, shuffle yer shoulders. Good! Keep goin'! Lovely. You'd make a fine sweep's boy, you would. A bit more—nearly there—give us yer 'and . . ."

Down below, Prudence and Solly shivered in the cold nursery. Yet more soot came pattering down. Then . . .

"Right!" came Freddy's voice. "She's out. 'Oo's next?"

"Ladies first," said Solly.

"Are you sure?" said Prudence. "You might need a kick up the—"

"I won't. I'm fine. Go."

And up went Prudence, leaving Solly all alone in the dark.

He could hear Freddy shouting down words of encouragement, but he didn't really take them in. His heart was beating too loudly. His mouth was dry. His hands were sweating. He ran a finger around the collar of his sailor suit, which seemed to be getting tighter by the second.

What if he panicked? What if he got stuck?

What if they lit the fire in the morning and he was still up there? What if—

"Come on, Solly!" came Prudence's muffled voice. "It's not that bad. Hurry up—it's freezing up here!"

Well. What was he to do? He took a deep breath, stepped into the grate, and looked up. Nothing but blackness. It was cold, too. A bitter draft played around his shoulders.

He couldn't do it. He knew it all at once. Shameful, but true.

"I can't do it," he called.

There was a short pause and muffled voices.

"Don't be silly," called down Prudence. "Rosa-bella and I did it."

"Yes, but that's different. She's got Mr. Skippy back and you've got your pencil."

"I don't see your point."

"So you've both got something to be cheerful about. I haven't. Anyway," he added rather feebly, "I don't feel well. So I can't do it. Go on without me, I don't care."

Then, "Sumfin's comin' down," called the Prodigy. "It's a suppwise!"

Something did come down. It landed softly on his head. He reached up.

It was his cloth.

"She got it from the fireplace and stuffed it up her knicker-leg," came Prudence's voice. "Get a move on, why don't you!"

Solly stood feeling his cloth in the dark. My, it felt good. Scorched around the edges, perhaps— but good. He made a mental note to buy the Prodigy the biggest bag of sweets in the world, once he came into his own and got rich.

Carefully, he folded it and stuffed it down his sailor suit, next to his heart. Suddenly everything was different. He was a boy with a napkin—and, somewhere out there, a silver spoon awaited him.

"Right," he called. "Here I come."

And he pressed his back firmly against the filthy bricks, wedged his knees against the opposite side, and began to climb the chimney.

The first thing that happened was that both his trouser legs split at the knees. Then a clump of soot fell from on high into his lap. Some went up his nose, and he sneezed. His head jerked back and collided with a sharp brick, which was sticking out.

"That's it!" came Freddy's voice. "Now shuffle yer shoulders!"

Solly tried to shuffle his shoulders up. There came a tearing sound, and his sailor suit split up the back and ruffled up around his shoulders. It seemed to be caught on something.

"I think I'm caught on something!" he called.

"Come on!" ordered Prudence, patient as always. "We can't wait all night!"

"I'm trying, I'm trying!"

He pushed upward again. The cloth gave way, and his bare skin ground against the rough brick-work. His knees wobbled. He gasped, and more soot went in his mouth.

"Solly," came the Prodigy's voice. "If you huwwy up, I'll give you the last sweetie I been savin'. It's a wed one."

Gritting his teeth, Solly dug in his elbows and slithered upward a bit, scrabbling with his knees.

Shuffle shoulders. Shuffle knees. Shuffle shoulders. Shuffle knees. He was getting the hang of it now.

"Not far!" shouted Freddy. His voice sounded closer now.

"Come on, slowpoke!" screeched Prudence. "What's keeping you?"

Nothing can be worse than this, thought Solly, giving another heave. This time, the seat of his pants gave. In the dark, in agony, clothing in shreds, a sheer drop below. No. Nothing can be worse.

Hands reached down and grabbed the tattered ruins of his sailor suit. To his wild relief, he found himself being hauled up, out of the horror of the chimney . . .

. . . and into the teeth of a raging blizzard.

NOTHING BUT SILVER

〜

In which the Intelligent Reader
is introduced to Mrs. Irma Spindletrap
and learns of her obsession.

M

rs. Irma Spindletrap was a collector of fine silver. Well, she could afford it. She made a good living out of orphans. Orphans were big business, if you played your cards right.

Mrs. Spindletrap played her cards very well indeed. She was employed by the Board of Good Works, an offshoot of the parish council. She received a considerable amount of money to house and feed each orphan—thirty-four of them at the last count—and spent a minuscule amount of money actually doing it. She had been successfully cheating the Board for years. Nobody ever came around to inspect the place or find out how the money was being spent. And, of course, there were no parents to complain.

Mrs. Spindletrap had it all worked out. The orphans did all the jobs around the house, so there was no need for staff. They slept eight to a bed. They wore rags. They lived on pottage made from weeds in the garden, which they pulled up, chopped up, and cooked up themselves. Discipline was easy. The biggest orphans were promoted to monitors. Their job was to enforce the rules. The perks included turnip on Sundays, being allowed to pinch the smaller orphans until they cried, and better beds with an extra sheet.

Mrs. Spindletrap didn't live on pottage. She dined on chicken and milk pudding served on fine china in the comfort of her own parlor. Her meals were cooked and delivered by the Town's finest hotel and brought to her on a tray by one of the monitors. If they didn't trip up or spill things, she occasionally rewarded them with scraps and the chance to warm themselves for a moment by her blazing fire before scuttling back to the freezing dormitories.

Tonight, the supper tray was in the shaking hands of Ploot. He had only recently been promoted to monitor and wasn't sure what he was supposed to do.

"Put it down, Ploot," instructed Mrs. Spindletrap. "And stop shaking. You'll spill the wine."

"Sorry, Mrs. Spindletrap. Er, where shall I put it?"

"On the table, fool boy. Where do you think?"

Concentrating hard, Ploot wobbled his way to the table, eyes down, avoiding meeting her steely gaze. Plates clattering, he set the tray before her. Mrs. Spindletrap held out a hand and lifted a silver-domed cover from a bowl.

"Ah," she said, inhaling fragrant steam. "Cream of chicken soup. I expect you wish this was your supper, eh, Ploot?"

"Yes, Mrs. Spindletrap," drooled Ploot.

"Well, keep your nose clean and do as you're told and I'll give you the bowl to scrape. You'd like that, wouldn't you?"

"Would I!" breathed Ploot.

"I thought so. Wait outside the door. I'll ring when I'm finished."

Ploot was just making for the door when he was stopped in his tracks.

"What's this?" rapped Mrs. Spindletrap. Ploot turned. She was holding up a spoon.

"A spoon, Mrs. Spindletrap," said Ploot, nervously.

"A tin spoon, Ploot. This is *tin*."

She took the spoon in both hands and bent it into a U-shape.

"You see? It bends, Ploot. I don't eat with tin spoons."

"S-sorry." Ploot hung his head. He'd done it all wrong.

"I have my own cutlery, boy. I am a lady, and ladies use silver. Nothing but silver . . ." Her eyes softened for a moment and she dreamily stroked the silver dome. Then she jerked back to attention. "Understand?"

"Yes, Mrs. Spindletrap. Sorry."

"So go. I am displeased. You are no longer a monitor. No leftovers for you. For the next seven nights, you will sleep in the coal hole. And as of tomorrow, you're on door duty."

Hanging his head, Ploot shambled out.

Mrs. Spindletrap rose, went to the mantelpiece, and opened the lid of a small, polished rosewood box. Inside was a silver key. She then went to a large, mahogany-fronted cabinet, inserted the key in the lock, and threw open the doors.

Silver. Nothing but silver. Silver candlesticks. Silver bowls. Silver picture frames. Silver statuettes. And masses and masses of silver cutlery. Fish knives. Steak knives. Pear knives. Dessert forks.

Pickle forks. And spoons! Teaspoons, mustard spoons, sugar spoons, pudding spoons, spoons of every description.

Mrs. Spindletrap's hard eyes softened as she pored over her treasured hoard. Years, it had taken, to build it up.

"Ahhh," breathed Mrs. Spindletrap. "My shining beauties!"

How she loved silver. It was hard. It glittered with a cold light. It was satisfying to hold, to clean (always with the softest cloths), but best of all, to simply look upon. Let others collect gold, or precious gems. Give her silver anytime.

Most of all, she loved her cutlery. There was something about the luxurious taste and feel of silver in the mouth.

She reached in and selected her favorite spoon. She had picked it up from a pawnshop a year or so ago. Pure luck. Mrs. Spindletrap didn't usually shop in the back streets, but she had gone to pick up a runaway orphan who had led her quite a chase around the alleyways until she cornered him in a cul-de-sac with her spiked umbrella.

It was when she was marching the wretched little rascal back toward the main street that she noticed the dusty shop displaying the sign of the three balls. Her collector's instinct clicked in. She'd tethered the orphan to a lamppost and entered.

Who would have thought it? Among all the faded rags and junk, there it was. A silver spoon. Not too big, not too small. The sort of spoon that rich people gave their babies to suck when they were cutting their teeth.

Mrs. Spindletrap knew quality when she saw it. This was a superb specimen. Solid silver, clearly crafted by a master silversmith. Initialed, too. The letters *V.I.P.* were elaborately inscribed on the handle. Presumably the owner had fallen on hard times. Or, more likely, considering how inexpensive it was and the eagerness of the pawnbroker to get rid of it, the spoon had been stolen, probably from the baby's mouth.

Mrs. Spindletrap didn't care. It was hers now. Hers, for a paltry few shillings.

She breathed on the spoon, polished it on her black velvet sleeve, and stared at her distorted reflection in the back. Then she smiled a tight little smile, sat down, and began delicately eating her soup.

I HAVE SOMETHING BELONGING TO *YOU*?

ᴧ

In which our heroes make their way
to Thrift House and make the
acquaintance of Mrs. Spindletrap.

The next morning, the blizzard of the night before had blown itself out. A pale shaft of sunlight illuminated the snowdrift, which was piled high against the blackened wall of a warehouse overlooking a snow-choked alley.

The drift reached to the sill of a broken window.

From the window emerged a sooty head. Then a skinny, soot-blackened boy wriggled through and dropped lightly into the drift.

Then a smaller figure scrambled out. She had sooty, bedraggled ringlets which, in another lifetime, were golden. She was dressed in filthy blue and was holding a rabbit under one arm and a battered parasol in the other. A ragged old blanket hung from her shoulders. She was followed by a tall, gawky female figure wearing an ugly straw bonnet with a pencil sticking out of it and a shabby brown cloak. Finally, a fourth figure emerged, wearing a thin jacket, shabby breeches, and an old cloth cap. A scorched piece of cloth was knotted around his neck.

All four waded out of the drift and stood in a huddle, shivering and looking around. There was an unnatural hush about the world, as only a heavy fall of snow can bring.

"Now what we gonna do?" said the Prodigy.

"We have to go to Thrift House and pay a visit to Mrs. Spindletrap," said Prudence. "We have to ask about Solly's spoon."

"I'll take you there," offered Freddy.

"I think perhaps you've helped enough," said Prudence. "We'll manage from now on."

"Might as well. Ain't got no job now."

"Perhaps Jonas Scurvy will take you back."

"But I don't wanna go back. I wanna come with you. Please!"

"Let him," said the Prodigy.

"All right," said Prudence grumpily.

"Listen," said Solly. "I've been thinking. Perhaps I should go on my own."

"Oh?" said Prudence. "Why?"

"Because you've already gotten into enough trouble because of me."

"True. But we might as well see it through to

the bitter end," said Prudence. "Then we can see if it was all worth it. I'm looking forward to seeing you in velvet pantaloons."

"I's comin' wiv you, Solly," said the Prodigy firmly. "You need me an' Mr. Skippy to hold your hand if you's scared."

"I'm not scared," said Solly.

"You was last night, though, wasn't you?"

Solly thought back to the horrors of the night before. The terrifying ascent of the chimney. His emergence into a hideous black nightmare of bitter winds and stinging snow. Then the desperate escape over the slippery rooftops. Slithering. Feet scrabbling for purchase on the sloping tiles. Missed footing. Blind stumbling. Heart-stopping leaps from one roof to another. Getting dizzy, clutching onto Prudence for balance, and getting a sharp elbow in his stomach. Having his hands forcibly pried away from chimney pots. And finally finding out that the Prodigy had been lying all along about the last red sweet, which she had long ago eaten herself.

Still. He couldn't be too cross with her. She had held his hand throughout—and, he mustn't forget, she had saved his dear old crumb-catching cloth. And, somehow, by some miracle, they had made it down off the rooftops in one piece. Freddy had led the way, of course, skipping around the roofs like a mountain goat, completely indifferent to the appalling weather conditions.

After what seemed like a lifetime, they had finally climbed down a steep parapet onto a flat roof, where there was a broken skylight. One by one, they had lowered themselves down into a chilly black warehouse, which was used to store flour. There, their old clothes awaited them. After changing, they had used Freddy's last match to make a bonfire of the hated clothes that Nanny had dressed them in. The ruined sailor suit, the filthy white dress, and the even filthier green one had gone up in flames, to much rejoicing. Once that jolly little ritual was over, there was nothing else to do but wait out the night, huddled under piles of scratchy old flour sacks that made them sneeze.

"Yes," agreed Solly. "I was scared then all right. I admit it. I'm not good at heights."

For once, Prudence didn't taunt him with Bugless. He was grateful for that.

"Right," said Freddy. "Thrift House it is. I know a shortcut through the alleyways. Follow me."

He sped off.

"Does he have to *run* everywhere?" sighed Solly.

Shivering, they trudged off in his wake

Thrift House turned out to be a large, gaunt building set back from the main street. There were spikes on the railings and stout bars over the windows. Over the peeling door was a board with THRIFT HOUSE ORPHANAGE inscribed on it. A bell rope hung to one side.

"Here goes, then," said Solly. And he grasped the rope and pulled hard. Harsh jangling sounded from within. After a moment or two, a boy's pale, pinched face peered through the grating.

"Yes?" said the boy, staring.

"We'd like to see Mrs. Irma Spindletrap, please," said Solly politely.

"Got a 'pointment?"

"No."

"She don't usually see folks without a 'pointment."

"It's very important," insisted Solly. "We don't mind waiting."

"What shall I say it's about?"

"It's a private matter."

"I dunno," muttered the pinch-faced boy. "I'm in trouble already."

Solly gave the Prodigy a nudge.

"Go on, do it," he muttered.

The Prodigy raised her dirty little head, smiled her gap-toothed smile, and did the eyelash-batting thing.

"Please, nice boy," she said, adding dimples for good measure.

"Wait there," said the boy instantly. "I'll ask."

And he vanished. The Prodigy gave a smirk and said, "Easy."

"You really are sickening, Rosabella," said Prudence. She stamped her feet. "Brrr. It's freezing out here. I hope he's not long. Nanny'll have discovered we're missing by now. She'll probably send the Boys out looking for us."

Nervously, they looked up and down the street. The Town was now slowly waking up to a white world. A tribe of ragged boys armed with brooms and shovels was already hard at work, shoveling snow and spreading salt and grit.

"It's Jonas Scurvy I'm more worried about," said Freddy. "Got a terrible temper on 'im. If he catches sight of me, I'll be in for it. Larrikins!"

Just then, much to their relief, there came the sound of bolts and chains being unfastened.

"Keep Mr. Skippy hidden," Solly muttered to the Prodigy. "I've a feeling pets might not be welcome."

The heavy door creaked open and the pinch-faced boy peered out again.

"All right," he said. "She says she'll see you."

They trooped in, stamping the snow from their feet.

They found themselves in a dim hall. The walls and floor were made of stone. There were no pictures, no hangings or decorations of any kind. There was a strange, unwholesome smell about the place—damp, mildew, and the lingering scent of unwashed bodies.

A small girl in a drab gray smock was on her hands and knees, scrubbing the floor with the aid of a nearly bald toothbrush and bucket of filthy water.

"Nearly done, Alice?" asked the pinch-faced boy.

"No, Ploot," said the small girl, at the point of bursting into tears.

"Get a move on, then. You know what she said. No breakfast till you done it."

"Is you a maid, lickle girl?" inquired the Prodigy.

"No," sniveled the small girl. "Just an orphan."

"Then don't do it," advised the Prodigy. "Scweam. Scweam until they beg you to stop."

"She's doing a punishment," said Ploot. "Mulligan said she had to. He's Head Monitor. Pushed in the dinner line, didn't you, Alice?"

"So she has to clean the floor with a toothbrush? That's terrible!" gasped Solly.

"That's nothin'. You gets used to it. The orphans does all the work round 'ere," explained Ploot. "Fact is, we runs the place. Or the monitors do."

"Monitors?"

"The big ones. I was a monitor yesterday, but I ain't anymore. She made me sleep in the coal hole, 'cause I gived her a tin spoon. I didn't mean it. Nobody said."

"So what are you now? Now that you're a fallen monitor?" asked Prudence.

"Doorman," said Ploot gloomily. "It's one of the worst jobs. You just stands on yer own next to the door all day. No one ever comes. Mrs. Spindletrap don't encourage visitors. I'd sooner be back on kitchen duty. You gets to lick the pot out."

Two small boys came hurrying along, carrying trays laden with empty wooden bowls. They stared briefly at the newcomers, then scuttled off along a dark passageway. Somewhere, a door squeaked open, then slammed shut.

"How many children live here?" inquired Prudence.

"Thirty-four at last count," said Ploot.

"It's very quiet, isn't it?"

"No talking in the corridors. She's very strict about that, is Mrs. Spindletrap. It's one of the rules. Shhh, now. This is her parlor."

He stopped outside a door and gave a gentle tap.

"Enter," commanded a voice.

Ploot pushed open the door and in they went.

They found themselves in a comfortable room with stuffed chairs, thick rugs, and paneled walls. At one end there was a well-spread breakfast table. Seated behind it was a sour-faced woman with a tight gray bun. She wore a high-necked black dress. Silver rings glittered on her fingers.

Her cold, steely gray eyes swept over them like an icy wind.

"Well?" she demanded. "What's all this about? What's so urgent that a pack of urchins needs to disturb a lady at her breakfast? Come along, who's speaking?"

"Me," said Prudence.

"No," said Solly firmly. After all, it was his spoon. "Me."

He removed his cap, stepped forward, and gave a polite little bow.

"How do you do, ma'am?" he said.

"Better without unnecessary interruptions," snapped the good lady. "Come on, out with it. I hope you're not expecting charity. I don't take orphans off the street, if you're hoping for free board and lodging. Neither do I give handouts."

"No," Solly hastened to explain. "Not charity. It's just that I think you may have something that belongs to me and I was rather hoping—"

"What?" Mrs. Spindletrap sat bolt upright. Her hard eyes bored into him. "Something belonging to *you*?"

"Well, yes. Of course, you wouldn't have known that, ma'am, I'm sure you bought it in good faith, but—"

"I have something belonging to *you*?"

"Yes. I think so. It's rather a long story, but when you hear it, I'm sure you'll—"

"A spoon," chipped in Prudence. She'd had enough of Solly's meanderings. She believed in getting straight to the point. "A silver spoon. You bought it from a pawnshop last November. You paid thirty shillings for it. It's engraved with the letters *V.I.P.* It's his inheritance, and he'd like it back."

Mrs. Spindletrap's jaw dropped open. She was speechless with shock. Never, in all her born days, had a child spoken to her like this.

"We can't pay you for it right now, I'm afraid," added Solly, "but we will, of course. Just as soon as we can. You see, I'm hoping to track down my real parents and . . ."

His voice trailed away. Mrs. Spindletrap had risen to her feet. Her mouth was a thin, white line. She raised her arm and pointed to the door.

"Out!" she spat.

"But if I could just explain—"

"Out! Coming here with your ludicrous story, trying to cheat me out of property! Out, before I call the police!"

"But at least you can tell us if you've got it, surely?"

"None of your business. Out. Now!"

"Come on," muttered Ploot. "Best be goin', eh?"

Silently, they turned and filed from the room.

SPOONS?
GOT 'EM COMIN' OUT HER EARS!

❧

In which the Intelligent Reader

will learn of our heroes' cunning plan

to remain in Thrift House

and mingle with the orphans.

S ee?" muttered Ploot as they walked back along the passageway. "I coulda told you you wouldn't get nowhere."

"How do you bear it here?" asked Prudence, staring around in disgust. "It's like a prison."

"No choice," said Ploot, with a sigh. "It's either this or beggin' in the streets."

"I like beggin' in the stweets," the Prodigy informed them. "I's good at it." Everyone ignored her.

They had almost reached the hallway. There was no sign of the small scrubbing girl. Just a great stretch of wet floor and the sturdy front door. Once they were out, that would be it. There would be no return.

"Look," said Solly, "we can't just leave like this. I refuse to believe this is the end of the line. We've not come all this way to—to just give up, surely?"

The five of them came to a halt.

"He's right," said Freddy.

"He is," agreed the Prodigy.

"I know," said Prudence.

"Come on," said Ploot uncomfortably. "You gotta go. You heard her."

"What to do, though?" mused Prudence, ignoring him. "We asked; she refused. We don't even know for sure she's still got the spoon."

"Oh, she'll have that all right," said Ploot. Everyone looked at him.

"How do you know?" asked Solly.

"She's got a cabinet full o' silver. I seen it through the keyhole. She didn't know I seen it, but I did. She takes this key from a box on the mantel. Then she goes to the cabinet and she throws it open. I tell you, I was fair blinded. Spoons? Got 'em comin' out her ears!"

"You see?" said Solly. "We've got to think of a plan. Come on, come on. What would Bugless do?"

Prudence reached up, took out her pencil, and began to chew.

"Who's B—?" began Ploot, but the others shushed him. Prudence needed time to think.

From somewhere deep within the house, there came the sound of a gong. This was followed by the distant sound of pattering footsteps.

"Seven o'clock," said Ploot. He looked a bit panicky. "Breakfast. Can't be late. I gotta go. Don't wanna rush you, but . . ."

"Does Mrs. Spindletrap come out of her parlor much?" inquired Prudence.

"No," said Ploot. "Not on cold days, anyways. It's the only room with a fire. The rest of the place is like an icebox. Look, you gotta go."

"Bugless would refuse to leave," said Prudence suddenly. "He'd stick around. He'd befriend a passing orphan and persuade him or her to help him pass himself off as a new boy and cunningly mingle, listening and watching and keeping a low profile until he saw his opportunity to sneak into old Spindletrap's parlor and make off with the spoon."

Everyone thought about this.

"Larrikins," said Freddy admiringly. "'Ow does she come up with it?"

"It's good," said the Prodigy. "Clever Pwudence. What's minglin'?"

"It's when you join in with the crowd," explained Prudence.

"And nobody's supposed to notice that three strangers have showed up? And are madly mingling all over the place?" inquired Solly.

"Why should they care?" said Prudence with a shrug. "As far as they're concerned, we're just some new orphans. Stop looking so dubious. It's a plan, isn't it?"

Privately, Solly thought the plan horribly vague. But it was all they had.

"I suppose it might work," he said cautiously, "if we could find an orphan to befriend."

Ploot suddenly found himself the focus of eight eyes.

"What?" he said uneasily.

"You heard us," said Prudence. "We're befriending you."

"I dunno about that," said Ploot, backing away.

"I'm afraid you haven't got any say in the matter. We need a sympathetic orphan on our side, and you're it. You're going to help us steal Solly's spoon."

"You're crazy," said Ploot. "Stark raving mad, the lot of you."

"Hey," said Prudence. "That's no way to talk about your new friends."

"I ain't your friend!"

"Yes, you are. Isn't he, Solly?"

"You are," said Solly, adding, "Sorry."

"But what if Mrs. Spindletrap finds out?"

protested Ploot, wringing his hands. "You don't know her. She's the very devil when crossed."

The Prodigy decided to take the matter into her own hands. She took Ploot's hand and stared up at him with her big blue eyes. Then she put her rosebud mouth to Ploot's rather large left ear.

"If you'll be our fwiend," she whispered, "I'll tell you a secwet."

"What?" said Ploot.

"I got a wabbit under my blanket."

"Yeah?" said Ploot, enchanted. "Let's see."

The Prodigy twitched her blanket to one side, revealing Mr. Skippy.

"Ah," said Ploot. "Look at that."

"He's called Mr. Skippy," confided the Prodigy. "He says he likes you."

Ploot reached out and stroked Mr. Skippy's head. "Never had a pet," he said. "Not allowed 'em in here."

"So that's settled," said Prudence firmly. She stuck her pencil back in her bonnet. "All friends. Don't worry, Ploot. I'm sure you'll learn to love us. Lead on."

"Where to?"

"The dining room. We've got to practice mingling. And we don't want to miss breakfast, do we?"

The dining room was a long, cold hall set with rough wooden tables and benches on which groups of ragged children sat in complete silence. Each clutched a small wooden bowl. Their eyes were fixed hungrily on a huge copper pot at one end. Several of the smaller children were drooling. Two bigger children—a tall, sullen-looking girl and a big, freckly boy—stood behind the pot, wearing aprons and holding large ladles.

"Mulligan an' Big Rosie," muttered Ploot as they sidled through the door, trying to look inconspicuous. "Head Monitors."

On the wall, dominating the room, was a huge ticking clock. The hands had almost reached seven.

There was an air of breathless anticipation. So strong was the lure of the clock that nobody even glanced at the newcomers. Ploot slid onto a vacant bench and beckoned.

"Sit here an' keep mum," he muttered. "If anyone asks, let me do the talkin'."

The clock began to chime. On the first stroke,

the freckly boy in the apron removed the lid of the pot. A familiar smell filled the air.

Solly gave an inward groan. Pottage. There was no mistaking it. Funnily enough, though, he suddenly felt a sharp pang of homesickness. What were Ma and Pa doing now? Had they let the pig move in again? Were the deliveries backing up?

He hoped they were all right.

The sullen girl pointed sternly with her ladle. Instantly the children on the table nearest the front shot to their feet and formed a line. The biggest ones were at the front. Monitors, probably. Alice, the tiny scrubbing girl, was there, waiting meekly at the back. She had clearly learned her lesson.

The line shuffled forward, each child receiving a small portion of green slop before scurrying back to the bench and digging in with gusto.

The little scene was repeated several times as various tables took their turn. Throughout the whole procedure, nobody spoke. The only sound was the scraping of benches, the shuffling of bare feet, and the desperate scraping of spoons.

Finally, it was their turn. At the given signal, the five of them rose, picked up their bowls, and moved to the front.

"Who's this?" asked the freckly boy with a glare.

"New kids, Mulligan," said Ploot.

"Mrs. Spindletrap never said."

"Only arrived this morning. She says to give 'em breakfast."

The boy gave a shrug and reluctantly dumped a small amount of pottage into their bowls. His eyes watched them as they made their way back to the bench.

"He's fed up because there ain't so much left in the pot for him to scrape out," muttered Ploot.

The five of them picked up their spoons and commenced eating the horrible breakfast. Three mouthfuls later, they had finished.

"Larrikins!" said Freddy, happily smacking his lips. "That hit the spot."

"You don't ask much from life, do you, Freddy?" said Prudence.

"Nope. That were a feast, that were. It's an orful place right enough, but say what you like, the food's good. What d'you reckon, Solly? Enjoy it? I know I did."

Solly stared at him in wonderment, then shook his head. Pottage was pottage. There was nothing more to say.

PERFECT PARENTS
INTERLUDE SIX

———————◆———————

In which the Intelligent Reader

is invited to attend

a rather grand dinner party,

hosted by Lord Charles

and his grieving wife.

"A fine meal, Charles," commented Lord Humphrey Tweezle, sitting back and dabbing his mustache with a napkin. "The roast mallard in particular. Haven't tasted anythin' so flavorsome since broiled lion, when Ai was in the Congo. Mai compliments to the chef."

"Oh, yes, ours too," twittered the Heyho sisters, fluttering their ostrich-feather fans.

Fat, red-faced Sir Channingpot Crisply and his tiny wife agreed, and so did the Chumpingtons. The meal had, indeed, been a triumph.

Lord Charles signaled to Barnacle, the butler, who stepped forward with more wine. Only Lady Elvira declined. She had been very quiet throughout the evening and had hardly touched her food.

"Go on, darling," urged her husband. "Have a little drop. It'll do you good."

"No thank you, Charles," said her Ladyship. "I fear I have another of my headaches coming on." She raised tragic eyes to the assembled guests. "Forgive me if I am *dull company. But it is on evenings like this, when we're all happily gathered around a groaning table, that my thoughts are drawn to my darling boy. Does he have anything to eat, I wonder?"*

An awkward little silence fell. Everyone present knew the tragedy of Lord Charles and Lady Elvira's only child, who had been stolen as a baby. It tended to put a damper on social occasions. Colonel Chumpington and Sir Channingpot Crisply exchanged guilty glances, both wishing they hadn't had seconds of pudding.

Lord Tweezle gave a little cough and said, "Still no news, Ai take it?"

"Afraid not, Tumpty," said Lord Charles heavily. "We examine the papers every day, of course. And we're always on the lookout for spoons. Occasionally we see one advertised and go racing off to inspect it, but thus far, we've drawn a blank."

A tear trickled down Lady Elvira's pale cheek.

"His little spoon," she murmured. "His dear little

engraved spoon, which I myself placed between his precious lips."

"Tregic," sighed Lord Tweezle.

The gentlemen rumbled their agreement, and the ladies made soothing noises. Before long, they ran out of appropriate sounds and another awkward little silence fell. The Heyho sisters fluttered their fans. Little Lady Channingpot Crisply knocked over a glass with her elbow and apologized profusely to Barnacle, who mopped up the mess in silence.

"Tell us what you've been doing since your return from foreign parts, Tweezle," suggested Sir Channingpot Crisply, in an attempt to bring some jollity back to the party. "I hear you've become interested in the affairs of the Town. Sitting on the parish council, by all accounts."

"Indeed," agreed Lord Tweezle. "Ai've taken it upon meself to find out how the money is being spent. Appallin'ly run, these councils. The Bawd of Good Works in particular. Fools have no idea how to hendle the funds."

"Takes an aristocrat to know how to do that," remarked Colonel Chumpington, to loud agreement.

"Oh yes," said Lord Tweezle. "Ai shall be makin' some changes, all right. As a matter of fact, tomorrow morning Ai intend to pay a surprise call on the lady who runs the local orphanage. Quaite frankly, Ai suspect sharp practice. Amount she charges per head, little tykes must be livin' on jem and caviar."

"Or imported broiled lion steaks, eh?" quipped Colonel Chumpington, chuckling.

Loud laughter greeted this.

"Well, I'm quite sure you will get to the bottom of it, Lord Tweezle," simpered the tallest Heyho sister.

"I will," agreed his Lordship. "No flies on me, ma'am."

"Hopefully, none on the lion steaks, either," said Colonel Chumpington with a chortle, hoping for another laugh. He got one, but it wasn't that loud.

"So," said Lord Charles. "Perhaps the ladies would

like to retire to the drawing room. What d'you say, my dear? Will you lead the way?"

But Lady Elvira merely stared into the distance, lips trembling, and murmured, "His little spoon . . ."

"You'd need more than a spoon to tackle a lion steak, eh, Tweezle?" contributed Colonel Chumpington, desperately milking it for all he was worth. This time, no one even tittered.

"It must be fascinating work, sitting on the council," said Lady Channingpot Crisply, clutching at a straw. "Do tell us all about it, Lord Tweezle."

At this point, Lady Elvira excused herself and went to bed.

MA'AM, YOU ARE A SAINT

༒

In which we rejoin our heroes
back at the orphanage,
Mrs. Spindletrap successfully
pulls the wool over Lord Tweezle's eyes,
and the Prodigy seizes her chance.

H

ow much longer we got to stay here?" complained the Prodigy the next morning. " 'Cause I's fed up bein' an orphan. I want to go an' buy sweeties."

Solly, Prudence, and the Prodigy were clustered at the end of a long, chilly passageway. Each was holding a broom. Big Rosie had put them on sweeping detail. This, apparently, was an unpopular chore, and as such, fell to the newest orphans. The brooms were old and almost bald. It was backbreaking work. Mind you, as Ploot pointed out, it wasn't as bad as door duty. At least they could stay together. And the constant moving around kept them relatively warm. Plus it meant that they could take turns spying on Mrs. Spindletrap's closed door without drawing undue attention.

"Stop whining, Rosabella," said Prudence. "You know we can't leave without Solly's spoon. We agreed."

"But I doesn't like it here. I's starvin'. All we do is work. An' nobody talks. I fink they hates us."

This was true. Life at Thrift House seemed to consist of nothing but an endless round of dreary chores, broken only by breakfast (pottage), supper (pottage again, with a small crust of bread), and bed. Nobody talked much.

"They don't hate us," explained Solly. "They're just too wrapped up in their own misery to care."

"Well, I want to leave," sulked the Prodigy. "I don't like pottage. It's gween. An' I don't want to sleep in that ol' bed again, wiv all them orphans what I doesn't know. I wanna sleep wiv Mr. Skippy. When can we go an' buy sweeties?"

"You are such a moaner," snapped Prudence. "We're all having a hard time of it, not just you."

The Prodigy was right, though. The sleeping arrangements left a lot to be desired. There were two icy dormitories situated at the very top of the house, one for the boys and one for the girls. Each contained two hard double beds for the smaller orphans and two single ones for the Head Monitors. Newcomers had to sleep on the outside edges of the larger bed and spend all night clinging on and fighting for a sliver of sheet while their bedfellows snored and thrashed around and shouted out in their sleep.

All of them had had a terrible night, apart from Mr. Skippy, who had bedded down in the coal hole with Ploot. The Prodigy was unhappy with the arrangement, but had given in, under pressure. Keeping him hidden while sleeping in a bed with seven others would have proved impossible.

Just then, Freddy came hurrying along from the direction of Mrs. Spindletrap's parlor, trailing a broom behind him.

"Any movement?" asked Solly hopefully.

"No," said Freddy. "Big Rosie came an' took 'er breakfast tray, that's all."

"She must come out eventually, though, mustn't she?" said Prudence. "She can't stay cooped up forever. She'll take a walk, or go out visiting or shopping or orphan-collecting or something."

"I wish you wouldn't talk like that," said Solly. Prudence could be really hardhearted at times. As usual, she ignored him.

"Then we can slip in, get the spoon, and leave this beastly place forever."

"Just a small point," said Solly. "What if she locks up behind her?"

"Cripes!" Prudence looked stunned. "You're right. She won't take any chances with a cupboard full of silver. Bother! I never thought of that. It seemed so easy when I said it."

"Maybe there's a spare key, like there was at the pawnbroker's," suggested Solly. "Ploot might know."

"Somebody else'd better take my place spyin'," said Freddy. "Big Rosie saw me 'angin' round an' told me to clear off."

"I'll go," offered the Prodigy, adding, "an' I isn't a moanin' Minnie."

She trailed off with her broom, looking crest-fallen.

Ploot stood yawning at his station by the front door. It was the coldest place in the house, and he was bored out of his mind. His limbs were stiff from sleeping in the coal hole. Waking up with a rabbit sitting on his head hadn't helped.

He was almost nodding off where he stood when a harsh jangling brought him to with a start. Hastily, he pulled back the grating shutter and peered out, hoping that it wasn't another bunch of weird kids wanting to befriend him and rope him into their dangerous games.

A haughty-looking gentleman with interesting side whiskers was staring back at him through a monocle. He wore an expensive overcoat and a top hat.

"Open the daw," instructed the gentleman.

"Who shall I say's callin'?" asked Ploot.

"Lord Humphrey Tweezle. Ai wish to see Mrs. Spindletrap."

"Have you got a 'pointment?"

"Ai do not require an appointment. Ai'm from the Bawd of Good Works. Open the daw."

"Wait there," said Ploot. "I'll ask."

The Prodigy was skulking in the passageway outside Mrs. Spindletrap's firmly closed door when she'd heard the front doorbell ring. After a few moments, there came the sound of fast approaching footsteps.

The Prodigy seized her broom and ducked around a corner.

She heard Ploot's panting breath, followed by an urgent knock. She heard the parlor door open, then close again. From behind it came the sound of muffled voices. The door opened again. Two sets of footsteps receded into the distance.

The Prodigy risked a look down the long passage. Empty. The parlor door stood ajar.

Perfect.

"Lord Tweezle!" cried Mrs. Spindletrap, throwing open the front door and dropping a low curtsy. "What an honor to meet you, sir. I was hoping you might find time in your busy schedule to visit our humble establishment."

"Ma'am," said Lord Tweezle stiffly, raising his hat and giving a slight bow.

"Take his Lordship's hat, Ploot, dear. Whatever were you thinking of, leaving him to stand out in the snow? You silly little sausage." Mrs. Spindletrap sighed and gave Ploot a kindly pat on the head. "Forgive him, sir. He so wanted the chance to stand at the door and welcome all the fine ladies and gentlemen that come a-calling. So excited, he couldn't eat the fine ham and fresh farm eggs provided for breakfast. And I was too softhearted to say no."

"Hem and eggs?" inquired Lord Tweezle with a little frown. "Is that usual, ma'am?"

"Oh yes, your Lordship. Nothing but the best for my charges. I wouldn't have it otherwise, sir.

Ham and eggs for breakfast and roast chicken for supper. And it's all thanks to the Board of Good Works and their generosity."

"Quaite," said Lord Tweezle. "Now then, ma'am, Ai won't beat about the bush. Ai am here on business. The Bawd appears to have been throwin' a great deal of money your way, ma'am. Ai've been studyin' the account books and quaite frenkly—"

"Not another word, sir!" interrupted Mrs. Spindletrap. "I won't hear it!"

"Eh?" exclaimed Lord Tweezle, taken aback.

"You shall not utter one more word until you're comfortably seated in my parlor with a glass of sherry. It's the very least I can offer. The parish must be delirious with joy. A fine gentleman like yourself, taking an interest in the Town's affairs. Delirious with joy!"

"Well, Ai wouldn't go quaite thet far—"

"Oh, don't be coy, your Lordship. You know it's true. You have quite a reputation, sir. It'd be a foolish person indeed who would try to pull the wool over your eyes."

"Well, Ai—"

"So educated. So well traveled."

"Well, Ai suppose Ai am rather—"

"The Congo, I hear. So brave. So intrepid. What tales you must have to tell. Come in, sir, come in and welcome. My, what a fine overcoat. You have an eye for a good weave, if you'll forgive my being so bold. Ah, what it is to be a gentleman of style and breeding. This way, your Lordship."

Round one to Mrs. Spindletrap. She really did play her cards well.

A short time later, Lord Tweezle sat drinking a third glass of sherry in Mrs. Spindletrap's parlor. He found he was enjoying himself. The sherry was good, and Mrs. Spindletrap was an excellent listener. Indeed, she hung on his every word. It was becoming clearer by the minute that he had been wrong about her cheating the Board. The woman was charming and clearly devoted to her charges.

"A little more, your Lordship?" asked Mrs. Spindletrap as he came to the end of an amusing story about crocodiles.

"Thenk you." His Lordship nodded. "Very faine sherry, ma'am."

"I'm glad you think so, sir," said Mrs. Spindletrap, sloshing it in. "I drink very little myself. Every penny I receive goes into the mouths of my family. That's how I think of my orphans, sir. One big, happy family."

"Very commendable," said Lord Tweezle. "Er, where are they all? The orphans?"

"Happily going about their quiet business, sir. In the mornings, they do a little light housework, just to keep themselves busy. They love helping around the place. A busy child is a joyful child."

"Oh, indeed," agreed Lord Tweezle, who knew nothing about children.

"Later, I shall take them to the park and let them play happily in the snow. To work up their appetites for tea. Muffins and jam, with plenty of good, fresh milk. Oh, if you could only see their grateful little faces. Poor, motherless little lambs."

"Ma'am," said Lord Tweezle, suppressing a hic-cup, "you are a saint."

He took a large silver watch from his waistcoat pocket and examined it rather woozily. He had been here longer than he had intended.

"I do my best, sir," said Mrs. Spindletrap demurely. "More sherry?"

"Well—er—"

"It will keep the cold out."

"Perhaps I should check on the orphans. . . ."

"Please. It's not often I entertain a gentleman from the Board. Just one. To please me."

"Well, perhaps one more for the road."

Lord Tweezle held out his glass. Mrs. Spindletrap poured. Lord Tweezle drank.

"A fine watch, your Lordship," remarked Mrs. Spindletrap. "Solid silver, if I'm not mistaken."

"It is, ma'am," agreed his Lordship.

"Beautiful. Truly exquisite."

"Fond of silver, are you, Mrs. Spindletrap?"

"I am, your Lordship. If I were a rich woman"— Mrs. Spindletrap sighed—"which, sadly, I am not, on account of spending every penny on the dear orphans, but if I were, I would treat myself to the odd little piece from time to time. As it is, I have to content myself with looking through shop windows."

"Indeed." Lord Tweezle thought of something. "Never noticed a small silver spoon, by any chance, in your travels?"

"A spoon, sir?"

"Yes. I was havin' dinner with some old friends of mine last night. Lord and Lady Parquet-Fflauring, of Hightowers Manor. Their only son and heir was stolen from his cot some years ago.

Suckin' on an engraved silver spoon. Shockin' affair. They've been searchin' for the spoon ever since, hopin' it might lead 'em to the missin' boy."

"What a tragedy," sighed Mrs. Spindletrap. "I think I recall reading something about it in the papers. No, sir, I cannot say I've ever seen such an item. Another little splash?"

"No, ma'am." Lord Tweezle rose to his feet, rather unsteadily. "Ai must be on my way. Ai present my repawt to the Bawd at noon."

"I trust it will be favorable, your Lordship?" asked Mrs. Spindletrap.

"Oh, indeed. It's very clear that you run an impeccable establishment. Your charges must consider themselves very fortunate to find warmth and shelter under your roof."

"I love them like they're my own, sir," said Mrs. Spindletrap demurely. "Let me show you to the door."

She left the room, with Lord Tweezle lurching in her wake.

After a moment or two, the velvet drape hanging before the window gave a twitch. Cautiously, the Prodigy stepped out from her hiding place. She tiptoed to the door, looked out—then made a run for it.

WE'S TWAPPED!

In which the Prodigy proves useful
and our heroes leave the orphanage,
only to find themselves
in another pickle.

Solly, Prudence, and Freddy were wearily at work brushing down the main staircase when the Prodigy came flying up waving her parasol, her face flushed with triumph.

"Solly!" she gasped. "I gotted it! I gotted your spoon!"

"What?" Solly's heart missed a beat, and he dropped the broom he was holding. "Really? How? Where?"

The Prodigy fumbled in her knicker-leg.

"Here," she said proudly, holding out her hand. Solly looked.

There it was. At long last. His silver spoon. The one he had been dreaming about for so long.

"Doesn't you want it?" said the Prodigy.

Slowly, Solly reached out and took it. It was heavier than he had expected. He turned it over in his hand. Small, beautifully formed, with a pear-shaped bowl and a tapering stem decorated with an ornate leaf pattern.

"That's it, all right," said Prudence, peering over his shoulder. "See? *V.I.P.* That's you." She pointed to the end of the spoon, which had been flattened to make room for the three all-important letters.

"Larrikins, Miss Rosabella!" gasped Freddy. "You're a little wonder, you are."

"Yes," agreed the Prodigy, "I am. It was easy. She wented out an' I wented in an' I got the key fwom the box like Ploot said an' I opened the cab'net an' it was fulla ole silver stuff an' Solly's spoon was wight at the fwont an' I knowed it was his 'cause I sawd the letters an' I tooked it an' I locked the cab'net up an' I putted the key back an' then she came back wiv a man an' I hidded behind the curtain an' they did a lotta talkin' an' they said about the spoon an' I listened to what they was sayin' an' now I know who your pawents are."

Solly stared at her, open-mouthed. It was all too much to take in.

"Well, go on, then," said Prudence. "Don't keep us in suspense. Who are they?"

"Lord an' Lady Parkay-Flawin'. That's what the man said. Lord an' Lady Parkay-Flawin', an' they live at Hightowers Manor. Did I do good? Can we go an' buy sweeties now?"

• • •

Down in the cold hall, Ploot was still on door duty. The important visitor had finally departed. Mrs. Spindletrap had waved him down the path, shut the door, and let out a sigh of relief. She then cuffed Ploot's head and sailed back to her parlor, looking highly pleased with herself.

He looked around at the sound of hurrying footsteps. His new friends were approaching across the hall. All four of them looked flushed and excited.

"We're leaving," announced Prudence. "We've got Solly's spoon."

"Where's Mr. Skippy?" asked the Prodigy anxiously. "I need him back now."

"He's down in the coal hole," said Ploot. "But I ain't supposed to leave the door."

"We'll watch it for you," promised Solly. "If anyone asks, we'll say you've gone to the privy or something."

"But if Mrs. Spindletrap—"

"Ploot," snapped Prudence. "Are you an orphan or a mouse? Go and get that rabbit *now*."

Ploot was used to obeying instructions. He hurried off to get the rabbit.

Freddy slid the shutter over the grating to one side and peered out.

"Coast's clear," he whispered. "I'll draw the bolts, so we don't waste time."

Getting the door open was a noisy business. Bolts squealed. Chains rattled. Somebody would hear, surely. If they got caught now, just as the end was in sight . . .

Nervously, Solly fingered his precious spoon, which he had carefully wrapped in his napkin and stuffed deep into his pocket. Suppose Mrs. Spindletrap had discovered it missing. She might be along any second, demanding that they turn out their pockets. Then what? Would she summon the police or lock them up in some forgotten attic room and leave them to rot?

"Come on, Ploot," he muttered through clenched teeth. "What's he doing? Come on."

His heart pounded at the sound of footsteps. But, thankfully, it was only Ploot, with Mr. Skippy in his arms.

"Hooway!" squealed the Prodigy, and she ran to collect her beloved, who showed no sign of recognition.

"Come on," said Freddy, swinging open the door, which creaked on its hinges. "We'd best be off while the goin's good."

"Bye, then," said Ploot.

Solly stopped. He held out his hand. Ploot reached out, and they solemnly shook.

"Goodbye, Ploot," said Solly. "Thanks for everything. You were a big help."

"That's all right," said Ploot gruffly. "It was—sorta fun. I'll miss the rabbit."

"You can come with us, you know, if you like," offered Solly. From behind him, he heard an exasperated sigh. Prudence was rolling her eyes to heaven. He knew without even looking. But he had to ask. It was only fair.

"No," said Ploot. "I daresn't. You'd better go."

So they went. Ploot's pinched face watched them rather sadly through the grill.

Outside, the sun shone. Sparkling snow still lay in patches on the pavement. It was cold, but wonderful. Wonderful to be free again, away from that dark house and into the clean air.

"Now what?" said Freddy.

"We go to Hightowers Manor, I suppose," said

Solly, adding, "Of course, it would help if we knew where that was."

"I think we should head back to the center of Town," said Prudence. "We'll make inquiries. One of the wagoners might know. Come on."

On the main street, it was business as usual. The snow of the day before was finally melting. Everywhere was awash with dirty brown slush, but it didn't seem to put people off. The shops were open, and a steady stream of customers bustled in and out. The beggars were begging, the peddlers were peddling, the carts and carriages were trundling, and somewhere, someone with an accordion was playing a tuneless dirge. The crossing boys were still hard at work spreading salt and grit.

"It feels weird to be outdoors again, doesn't it?" said Prudence. "After days of being cooped up . . ."

But Solly wasn't listening. He had stopped in his tracks and was silently pointing at a lamppost, on which was displayed . . .

. . . a poster. A poster of the Prodigy, dressed all in blue, posing all pointy-toed and prettily dimpled, her most nauseating smile fixed firmly in place. The writing said:

MISSING SINCE TUESDAY

ANSWERS TO THE NAME OF LITTLE ROSABELLA

APPROACH WITH CAUTION

FIVE POUNDS REWARD FOR INFORMATION

"It's *you!*" hissed Prudence, turning accusingly on the Prodigy.

"I know," said the Prodigy, looking rather smug.

"A big huge picture of you, offering a reward!"

"I know."

"Larrikins!" gasped Freddy. "She's famous!"

"I know."

Then, just at that moment —

"Oh, no!" moaned Solly. "I don't believe this!" He was staring farther down the street, his face a mask of horror.

"What?"

"The Boys! They're heading our way."

Indeed they were. They were heading straight toward them, peering down side streets and checking doorways. And then, as if things weren't bad enough —

"RRRRRAAAAAAR!"

There came a terrible roar from behind them. It sounded like an enraged bull. Freddy gave a high-pitched squeal. A huge man stood in the street. He wore a battered stovepipe hat and filthy clothes. His eyes bulged. His fists clenched. His entire sooty being quivered with uncontrollable rage. He was like a kettle about to boil over.

"Larrikins!" gasped Freddy, going white beneath his soot. "It's Jonas Scurvy!"

"We's twapped!" wailed the Prodigy. "What we gonna do?"

Their desperate eyes scoured the street. A covered wagon was passing by, the horse straining and struggling for purchase in the slush.

It was their only chance.

The wagoner was relieved to be heading out of Town again. He was a countryman and couldn't believe the fuss they made about a bit of snow. All this griping nonsense got on his nerves. Where he lived, folks were hardy. They just shrugged and got on with things. Flood? Get a bucket. Blizzard? Get a shovel. Chop your toe off? Get a bandage.

The horse's hooves and the squeal of the wheels

rolling through slush made a terrible racket. He didn't hear the sound of running footsteps as four desperate, slithering figures came racing up behind and threw themselves over the tailboard into the back. Neither did he hear distant shouts and angry roaring as the pursuing hunters lost all hope of catching their prey.

He simply shook the reins and the horse pulled harder. Soon, the shops and houses were behind them and they were heading for deep countryside.

White hedgerows, white woods, quiet white hills. Here and there the snow was melting, but mostly it remained intact. It plopped softly from branches as the wagon jolted along, its heavy wheels leaving deep grooves in the pristine lanes.

Sometime later, the wagoner pulled on the reins and the sweating horse puffed to a grateful stop. The wagoner pulled out a pipe. The horse kicked some snow away and bent its head to nibble the grass beneath. All was peaceful and silent. Even the birds were still.

So the wagoner nearly set fire to himself with shock when he heard the singing.

"I's a little angel, flyin' thwoo the niiiight . . ." it went.

"What the tarnation . . ." gasped the wagoner, beating out the flames in his lap.

" . . . *Wiv my little halo, such a pwetty siiiight.*"

And a small, dirty girl suddenly appeared beside him, looked up with a pair of divinely blue eyes and said, "Hello, Mister Wagonman. I's Little Wosabella and I's lost. Please, oh, please will you take me to Hightowers Manor?"

OUR BOY!

A truly dramatic chapter
in which Solly meets with
the Perfect Parents
and all is finally revealed.

It was late afternoon, and Lady Elvira and Lord Charles were sitting in the drawing room. They had been quiet all day. The dinner party of the previous night had not been a success and had broken up embarrassingly early. Lady Elvira had apologized and promised to write notes. Lord Charles had said never mind, darling, he quite understood. And then they had run out of things to say.

They were on their third cup of tea when Barnacle made the announcement.

"I beg your pardon, Barnacle?" said her Ladyship. "Visitors, did you say?"

"Four urchins, my Lady. Asking to see you and his Lordship."

"Really? Do you hear that, Charles? There are urchins on the doorstep, asking for us. How very curious. Whatever can they want?"

"They wouldn't say, my Lady. But I thought you should know that one of them mentioned something about a spoon—"

Barnacle didn't get any further. Lady Elvira gave a sharp gasp and rose to her feet, all color draining from her cheeks.

"Charles!" she breathed, through trembling lips. "Oh Charles, can it be?"

"Now then, darling, don't jump to conclusions," said her husband, going to her side.

"Show them in, Barnacle," cried her Ladyship, trembling like a leaf, clutching her heart. "Oh, show them in, do!"

Solly, Prudence, Freddy, the Prodigy, and Mr. Skippy stood waiting beneath the columns, eyeing the towering front door.

"I suppose all this is yours," said Prudence to Solly, staring around at the sweeping grounds. "All this land. Think how rich you must be."

"Mmm," said Solly. He stared up at the house, then back at the grounds. What would it be like living here? He simply couldn't imagine.

"I can just see you skipping around the place in your purple pantaloons. Learning to play the piano. Having dancing lessons. Posing for your portrait."

"Stop teasin' him," said the Prodigy. "You's just jealous."

"No I'm not. Writers are creative people. We don't care about being rich."

"Larrikins!" said Freddy dreamily. "I'd like it, that's fer sure."

"It's very grand, I'll say that," said Solly, swallowing nervously. "Looking at the state of us, I'll be amazed if they let us in."

Their wild appearance certainly hadn't improved. A ten-mile ride in a wagon full of bags of mulch is guaranteed to add a few more travel stains, not to mention smells.

"Will they give us sweeties, do you fink? Your new pawents?" asked the Prodigy. She, of course, had ridden up front, singing to the wagoner, who had been only too pleased to take a huge detour and drop his enchanting little companion directly outside the gates.

He had been less pleased when he found out that he had unknowingly given a lift to three less enchanting others, especially the rude girl with the sharp nose, but by then it was too late.

"Don't you ever think about anything else?" scolded Prudence.

"Yes. I fink about how howwid you are sometimes," said the Prodigy with spirit, adding, "an' Mr. Skippy finks so too."

Solly sighed. Another argument was developing. He could have done without it. He was feeling nervous enough already. He fingered the spoon deep in his pocket. Just think. He was about to meet his real parents.

"Shhh," hissed Freddy. "'Ere comes the old geezer again."

The ancient butler appeared in the doorway and beckoned. Silently, they followed him in.

One look at the grand hall was enough to subdue them still further. High ceilings, wood-paneled walls, polished boards, deep rugs of darkest crimson, oil paintings, marble statues, gold leaf—it was more than they could take in.

The butler signaled for them to follow him down a long passageway. In silence, they complied. He paused at a door and knocked.

"Come in," called a tremulous female voice.

The door opened—and in they trooped.

The drawing room was light, spacious, and elegant, just as Solly knew it would be. But he wasn't really interested in the decor. His eyes were drawn like magnets to the two people who stood before the mantelpiece, which framed a blazing fire. A gracious lady in a gray gown, and a tall gentleman with a splendid mustache. Just like in his dreams.

Nobody said a word. This was Solly's big moment. He removed his cap, stepped forward, and gave a little bow.

Self-consciously, he cleared his throat. He had practiced this little speech many times in his head, but for some reason, he was finding it hard to deliver.

"Ahem. Lord and Lady Parkay-Flawin', I presume? Look, sorry to bother you, but it's rather important. You might want to sit down, because this will come as a shock. You see, I rather think I'm your missing s—"

But he was interrupted.

"Our boy!" cried the lady, her voice breaking with emotion. "Oh, Charles! It is! It's him! That little face! Those ears! Those eyes! That smile! I'd know him anywhere! My baby!"

And she ran forward, arms outstretched. Solly prepared himself for the inevitable embrace—

Which never came. Instead, she ran straight past him, and with a loud cry of maternal joy, gathered Freddy to her bosom!

"What?" said Solly.

"She's made a mistake," said Prudence. "Go on. Say something."

"Um, excuse me?" said Solly, trying to make himself heard above Lady Elvira's hysterical weeping. Freddy was still clutched tight in her arms, looking bewildered. Her tears were making channels in his dirty neck. To make things even more confused, Lord Charles was now getting in on the act and was attempting to wrap his arms around both of them.

"Leave them, lad," advised Barnacle, blowing his nose, shaking his old head, grinning, and wiping away tears all at the same time. "This is a reunion. Leave them to their joy. Oh, happy day!"

"But they've got the wrong *son*," explained Solly, fumbling deep in his pocket where his spoon had lodged itself in a hole or something. "It's not him, it's me!"

"Show him the spoon," said Prudence impatiently.

"I'm trying, I'm trying! It's stuck or something . . ."

"Oh, Rawthsea, Rawthsea, my little Rawthsea! How mother has missed you these last ten years!"

blubbered Lady Elvira, smothering Freddy with kisses.

"Who's Wawthsea?" asked the Prodigy, picking a leaf from the nearest potted plant and feeding it to Mr. Skippy.

"How should I know?" snapped Solly, still trying to extricate the spoon. He turned to the butler. "Who's Rawthsea?"

"Young Master Rawthsea, who was stolen from his cot ten years back," explained Barnacle. "Ah, 'twas a sad, sad day. My Lord and Lady have been seeking him ever since. And here he is, safe and sound."

"But he can't be called Rawthsea," said Prudence. "That doesn't begin with a *V*. What's his middle name?"

"Buckland. Little Lord Rawthsea Buckland Parquet-Fflauring. Snatched from his bed on the one day that all the doors were open because we were having the chimneys cleaned."

"But he had a silver spoon in his mouth, right?"

"Oh, yes."

"Right, then," cried Solly. "So what's this, then? If it isn't a silver spoon?"

Finally, with a ripping noise, the spoon came out. Triumphantly, Solly thrust it beneath Barnacle's nose.

"Well, yes," agreed Barnacle. "It's a spoon. But it's not Little Lord Rawthsea's. That says V.I.P. His said R.B.P.F. Rawthsea Buckland Parquet-Fflauring."

Just then, Lady Elvira gave a cry.

"Look! Charles! He has a mole under his ear! He had that when he was a baby!"

"So?" muttered the Prodigy. "I got a wabbit under my blanket."

Dumbfounded, Solly stared over at the joyful reunion scene, then down at the spoon in his hand.

The wrong spoon.

He simply couldn't believe it.

After everything he had been through.

How utterly, utterly awful.

So why, then, was he suddenly feeling this overwhelming sense of relief?

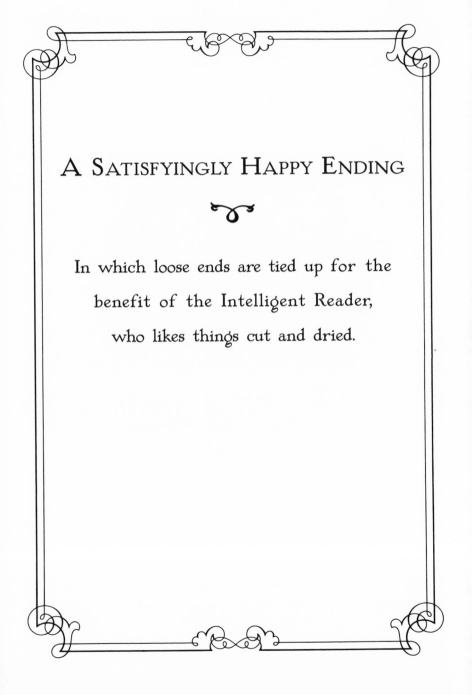

A Satisfyingly Happy Ending

In which loose ends are tied up for the
benefit of the Intelligent Reader,
who likes things cut and dried.

It wasn't exactly the wrong spoon," mused Prudence. "I mean, it was the spoon you set out to get in the first place."

"All right, so it didn't match the parents, then."

It was several months later. Solly and Prudence were sitting on the log under Prudence's tree, sharing a sandwich. Spring was in the air. Solly was on his way back from collecting Old Mother Rust's summer unmentionables.

Quite a bit of time had passed since the Business with the Spoon, as they now referred to it. Christmas had come and gone, and life was settling back into a routine. Solly was back delivering washing, and Prudence was back up her tree, rewriting *Little Sir Thummagain*.

Mind you, Christmas had been a good one, reflected Solly. There had been a turkey on the table, and plum pudding. The cat and the pig had had a field day. The reward money had seen to that.

"Do you care?" asked Prudence. "That Freddy turned out to be the missing son, not you?"

"No, not really. I've already got one set of wrong parents. I don't need another."

"The Parquet-Fflaurings didn't even offer to adopt you. I thought that was a bit mean. You're better off with the Scubbinses, in some ways."

"Mmm," said Solly.

He thought back to the Homecoming. Ma and Pa had been thrilled to see him and so had the pig. The cat had seemed indifferent. Ma had given him a hug, glanced at his *V.I.P.* spoon, dumped a load of pottage in his bowl, then sent him out to get water and chop logs before putting him to work folding sheets all night. Pa had celebrated by going to the tavern for a pint. They didn't even seem that interested in his adventures.

"They were pleased to have you back, weren't they?" said Prudence.

"Oh, yes. They were *desperate* to have me back. You should have seen the state of the place. The pig had moved in and Ma was days behind with the wash. I was back at work five minutes after walking through the door."

"That's nothing," said Prudence. "I had about

two minutes where they all said they missed me, then Ma gave me a slap for frightening her and made me wash all the little ones' ears."

"That's parents for you," agreed Solly. "They take us for granted."

They both sat reflecting on this.

"But for all that," said Prudence, "for all that, I don't envy Freddy."

They caught each other's eye.

"Those pantaloons," said Prudence. And they both gave a giggle.

Lord Charles and Lady Elvira had been very grateful for the safe return of their long-lost son. They clearly doted on Freddy, who indeed scrubbed up very well and fell into his new role as returned missing heir in no time. He even stopped saying "larrikins." He was clearly born to the role.

"The reward money was nice, though," said Prudence. "And the tea. And the coach ride home. It was nice to return in style."

The Parquet-Fflaurings had indeed been good hosts. They had insisted on Rawthsea's little friends having tea, cake, full access to the bathroom, and a substantial reward. They offered to let them stay for a few days, but Solly, Prudence, and the Prodigy had politely declined. Freddy seemed very happy wearing pantaloons, and Solly was happy to leave him to it. They felt a bit awkward hanging around in the grand house while Freddy/Rawthsea and his new mother and father got to know each other. Besides, Prudence wanted to get on with her writing, and the Prodigy wanted to go somewhere and buy sweets, then return to the circus and show Mr. Skippy off.

Lord Charles and Lady Elvira had paid for a coach to take them all the way home. Stopping off at the circus had taken a while. The second the Prodigy was back in the bosom of her family, she reverted to her former ways. She tossed her hair and grandly demanded things. She refused to share the sweets. She sulked and flounced. She showed off Mr. Skippy's trick of just sitting and announced that she was going to work him into her act. When Signor Madelini said she couldn't, she screamed and threw a temper tantrum.

Solly and Prudence were disgusted with her. They hung around trying to say goodbye, but the Prodigy wasn't interested. She was far too busy screaming. So they gave up. They claimed their five pounds' reward money from Signor Madelini, who rolled his eyes to heaven, sighed, and paid up. Then they climbed back in the coach and left the Prodigy to rave on.

Next it was on to Boring village, where Prudence was mobbed by her large, overexcited family.

Prudence had had a good Christmas, too. Lord Charles had used his influence to get her dad released from prison. There had been rabbit stew for dinner and new bonnets for all her sisters. Her little brother Cleanliness got three wooden soldiers, all of which he ate. Prudence treated herself to a new composition book. She still used the old pencil, though, Solly noticed.

They had both been so busy since then that they had only met a couple of times. Whenever they did, they had plenty to talk about.

Lady Elvira was an excellent correspondent. Perfumed letters in her own fair hand arrived regularly, keeping them up to date on developments. Solly couldn't read his, of course. He only knew three letters. *V, I,* and *P.* Prudence had promised to teach him the rest sometime, but it hadn't happened yet. He kept the correspondence in a tin box, along with his poor old cloth, which was fit for nothing now. It didn't really matter that he couldn't read them. Prudence told him all the important things.

Nanny and the Boys had been arrested. So had Jonas Scurvy. Mrs. Spindletrap had been fired from her position and a nice, kindly old lady called Mrs. Smiling had taken over Thrift House, which was now called Happy Home. The place now boasted fires in every room, apparently, and the orphans got chicken and apples and were allowed to play instead of work, so that was something. At Freddy's request, Ploot had been promoted to Head Boy.

"What I still don't understand is, what happened to Freddy's spoon?" mused Solly. "The one with *R.B.P.F.* on it?"

"Who knows?" Prudence shrugged. "Jonas Scurvy sold it, probably. Soon after he stole the baby. If he had any sense."

"That's another thing. Why steal a rich baby in the first place? If all you're going to do with it is shove it up chimneys for the next ten years?"

"Perhaps he thought he'd hold it for ransom, then decided against it."

"But why didn't the Parquet-Fflaurings put two and two together? Seeing as Freddy went missing on the very day they had the chimneys cleaned? Why rush about searching for a spoon for ten years when all they had to do was go to Town and seek out Jonas Scurvy? It doesn't make sense."

"What does it matter?" said Prudence. "A lot of things don't make sense. Why do you care?"

"I don't know. It's just nice to have all the ends tied up."

"That only happens in stories. Real life's not so neat. The plots are full of holes. The important thing is, you got your spoon. What do you do with it, by the way?"

"Use it to eat with. What do you think?"

"Right. So things have changed for the better."

"Mmm," said Solly. "Yes. I suppose they have. A bit."

Well, they had. Even after buying Ma a new ironing machine and Pa a large tin of back cream, there was still a bit of reward money left, so he would be able to buy himself a new pair of boots. And people treated him with a bit more respect, now that that he was a man of the world who had been to Town. And there was meat on the table from time to time, and fresh bread. Of course, it was only a matter of time before they were back to pottage again — but at least he now had a spoon to eat it with.

Prudence stood up, brushing crumbs from her lap.

"Got to get back to work," she said, eyeing her tree. Her new composition book was up there, stuffed into the hole.

"Right," said Solly. "How's it going, by the way? The book?"

"All right," said Prudence.

Losing an entire novel before it even reached the publishers hadn't put her off, it seemed. Whenever he came across her, she was scribbling. Nobody seemed to have insisted she go back to school, either. In fact, her dad seemed rather proud of the fact that he had a brainy daughter who made money and had aristocratic friends who got him out of jail. Although it didn't stop him from getting back to poaching.

"Well, tell me, then," Solly insisted.

"Well, it's different. I'm trying a different approach."

"Oh? How's Bugless getting on?"

"There is no Bugless. I've cut him out."

"What?" Solly was shocked. "You *dumped* him? Just like that?"

"Yes. He was rubbish, actually. I see that now. I'm working on a new central character. He'll be more real."

"How d'you mean, more real?"

"Well, a bit more like you. Obviously." Prudence spoke briskly, but the end of her nose went a bit red.

"Me?" Solly was astounded. "Me? Really? How?"

"I don't know. Does it matter?"

"Well, yes. Yes, it does. How is he more like me? Shorter? Straight hair or something?"

"No, not that. I mean more sympathetic. Kind. I'll give him good manners, like you."

"You mean he'll be a weakling," said Solly. "That's what you mean, isn't it?"

"No, I don't. I mean—nice. Somebody the reader will like. You're nice."

"Am I?" said Solly.

How odd. He hadn't thought he was.

"Yes. You are. You know, ever since we met, you've never once mentioned my nose."

"That's because I forgot about it."

"Exactly. You see? That's nice."

They were both getting a bit pink and flustered now. It was quite a strain, being pleasant to each other.

"Shouldn't you be delivering the washing?" suggested Prudence.

"Yes," agreed Solly gratefully, "I should." He stood and picked up the bag. "Did you get the circus tickets, by the way?"

"Yep," said Prudence. "All eleven of them. Arrived this morning."

"I'm looking forward to it, aren't you?" said Solly.

Well, he was. Just imagine. Free tickets, compliments of Signor Madelini. A proper family outing to a real circus. Ma and Pa were having a rare night off. A proper carriage was coming to collect them at nightfall and drive them in style to the field where Madelini's Marvelous Extravaganza was all ready and waiting. The Parquet-Fflaurings would be there with Freddy, so it was going to be a proper reunion, with a big supper after the show.

"It'll be nice to see Freddy," said Prudence. "But if Rosabella sings, I'm walking out, and I expect you to do the same."

"I will," promised Solly, although absence had made his heart grow fonder. He was looking forward to seeing the Prodigy. And even Mr. Skippy. He had a feeling that Prudence was, too.

"I'm off then," he said.

"Good," said Prudence. "See you later." It was clear she wanted to get rid of him.

Solly gave a little sigh and hoisted his bag onto his shoulder. It was a long walk home.

"What's the sigh for?" said Prudence. She was already back up in the tree, book and pencil at the ready.

"Nothing. It's just—well, nothing's changed much, has it? All that effort and here I am, back delivering washing."

"So? You've still got a mysterious past. And a whole different life out there, somewhere. Another set of parents, Lord and Lady Pucksnoot or something, seeking their dear little Verdigris Igor who got mislaid in a washing basket. Just think. A whole new adventure lies before you."

"Hmm," said Solly. He thought back to the last one. He remembered the endless walking, the painful boots, the relentless rain, the miserable barn, the frozen lips, the stifling nursery, the embarrassing

sailor suit, the flight across the rooftops, the blizzard, the orphanage, the mix-up with the spoon,
the—well, all of it.

"Actually," he said, "I think perhaps I'll leave
that for another time."

But Prudence had stopped listening.

So Solly set off for home. There was a spring
in his step, and he found himself whistling. All the
way back, he thought about the circus. That was
enough excitement for now.

And maybe the Prodigy will have taught Mr.
Skippy to jump through a flaming hoop.

Dear Intelligent Reader,

I congratulate you on reaching the final page of this thoroughly riveting tale—though please note that this is not the end of Solomon Snow's story. Soon you will be able to read all about his daring investigative exploits in *Solomon Snow and the Stolen Jewel*!

Prepare to **WONDER** as Solly solves baffling clues to track down an exotic treasure (yes, it's cursed), **TREMBLE** at the sinister surprises awaiting him at the circus, and **CHEER** as he outwits a dastardly criminal mastermind.

Indeed, some very strange happenings await our hero, along with his trusted companions, bossy Prudence, the awful Prodigy, and of course, Mr. Skippy. Come along on their next adventure— if you dare!

Yours in bejeweled mystery,

Kaye Umansky